LOST VICTIM

An absolutely gripping crime mystery with a massive twist

HELEN H. DURRANT

Detective Rachel King Series Book 6

JOFFE
BOOKS

Joffe Books, London
www.joffebooks.com

First published in Great Britain in 2023

ISBN: 978-1-80405-901-2

For my first great-granddaughter, Lola. My little bundle of fun.

PROLOGUE

Mary Dunn had to die. He'd thought about it long and hard, but could see no alternative. In the dim light of the gaunt stone church, the killer hid behind a pillar, waiting for his moment. He watched her flit around, arranging flowers, oblivious to her impending fate.

A small, nimble-footed woman, Mary didn't seem bothered by the growing darkness, or the fact that she was alone. The killer shivered. This place, and the violence he was about to do to an innocent old woman, were both alien to him. Normally, it would never have entered his head to perpetrate such an act. But things were not normal, far from it.

He wondered who would find the body. No doubt another member of the legion of female pensioners who tended the church. The police would be baffled. And they'd be right. After all, who'd want to kill a nice old lady like Mary Dunn? Mary was the last person you'd expect to fall foul of a murderer. She was a pillar of the local community with no enemies and little in the way of money or valuables. Nor, as far as the community was aware, was there anything in her past to make her a target.

Nothing but her curiosity. What was that saying? *Curiosity killed the cat.* It would certainly be the death of Mary.

The police would do their best. They'd visit her house on the terraced street just a few hundred metres away. Look at her life. Question her relatives and neighbours. Drawing a blank, they'd look at her past. From what little the killer knew of Ancoats, they'd learn that Mary had lived here all her life, and had known this place during good times and bad. Her friends would recount how she'd worked in the old cotton mill in the days before Ancoats became the sought-after area it was today, with its fancy eateries and sky-high property prices. The Ancoats that Mary had known was made up of large, greedy cotton mills that sucked up the local population, giving nothing in return but meagre wages and hard slog. It had been Mary's lot, and the lot of hundreds like her.

The killer shivered again. This place had an oppressive atmosphere that insidiously stole one's resolve. He told himself to focus, and remember why this had to be done.

Nerves honed, shaking hands steadied and grasping the razor-sharp dagger tight, he was ready. Time for Mary Dunn to breathe no more.

CHAPTER ONE

Sofia Nicolescu woke from a fitful sleep. Something was wrong. She had no idea how she knew — just call it intuition. As usual, the couple she worked for, Jacob and Lauren Gilbert, were arguing downstairs. Suddenly, Lauren screamed. Sofia raised her scrawny, aching body from the thin mattress and listened. She could hear the flat, northern voice of Jacob, laying into his wife for her latest misdemeanour. Not that Sofia blamed him. Lauren was a first-class bitch and deserved all the aggro she got.

The minutes ticked by. All at once, Lauren shouted up the stairs, "Get down here, girl. I need your help."

Sofia snatched up her robe and wrapping it around herself took the two flights of stairs down to the sitting room. She found Lauren sitting in an armchair, sipping wine as if nothing had happened. Jacob was nowhere to be seen.

"I heard a scream," Sofia said accusingly. "Is everything all right, madam?"

"No, it isn't. We're supposed to be going to friends for dinner, but one call to say the kid has been spotted and he takes off."

"The kid" was Emma Gilbert, Jacob's seventeen-year-old daughter. It was over a month since she'd run away and Jacob was desperate to get her back.

Lauren shook her head dismissively. "It'll be a false alarm. The girl's a liability, Jacob's better off without her. I try to tell him but he flies off the handle."

Having the three of them under this one roof was a recipe for trouble. Sofia was well aware that there was no love lost between Lauren and Emma — she was Jacob's daughter, not Lauren's.

"Well, there's no point in you going back to bed. As I said, I'm going out later and I'll need you to help me dress."

It was the last thing Sofia needed. She'd been working all day and was exhausted.

Lauren pointed to the stairs. "Up you go and run my bath — and get some clothes on while you're at it. I'm expecting a visitor and we don't want the help distracting him, do we?"

Sofia had long since given up complaining, it was a useless exercise. Lauren was a heartless bitch with a horrendous temper. She hated Sofia and the other trafficked girls her husband insisted on bringing into their home to work for them, while Jacob couldn't understand why Lauren was so dead set against them. Sofia had often heard him telling his wife not to be so stupid and what an asset they were. Cost and trouble-free he called them — in other words helpless slaves.

Every time she heard him say those words, Sofia grew more angry and bitter. This wasn't what she'd been promised. The men who had brought her and the others here had promised them independence, a decent place to live and a paid job so they could send money home. If she'd known the truth, Sofia would never have left Romania.

Upstairs, Sofia busied herself running the bath and tidying the bedroom. In the adjoining room, Lauren was on her mobile shouting at someone in her usual ill-tempered voice. Moments later, she swept into the bedroom, eyes blazing.

"Get on with it, girl. You're not paid to stand around gawping."

Paid? I'm not paid and you know it, Sofia wanted to retort, but she held her tongue. It was a fight she couldn't win. The Gilberts had the upper hand. Sofia had learned fast, soon coming to terms with having no redress. She kept her mouth shut.

It might be said that for a trafficked girl, Sofia had a pretty cushy number. Cleaning was easy compared to running drugs. She was out of the cold, there was no danger from the police or rival dealers, so what did she have to complain about?

In Sofia's opinion she had plenty to complain of. Lauren Gilbert took a particular delight in making her life a misery. She was riddled with jealousy, believing that the trafficked girls only got jobs in the house because they'd caught her husband, Jacob's, eye. The bitch was right. Jacob Gilbert did have an eye for the girls and, lovely as Lauren was, there was nothing she could do to stop it.

"I want my midnight blue and I'll wear the sapphires with it."

Sofia nodded obediently and went into the dressing room to find the gown. From the corner of her eye she saw Lauren on her mobile again, muttering angrily as she opened the safe in the bedroom.

"He's a fool," Lauren said. "A soft touch for any pretty face that takes his fancy. But you wait, I'll show him. That man is due the shock of his life."

Sofia gave a sly smile. Her philandering husband again.

"He's not the only one who can play dirty, others have people to fight their corner too."

Sofia waited until the call was over before returning to the bedroom. Obviously rattled, the woman now had a large gin in her hand. Lauren in a bad mood was bad enough but drink made her unpredictable.

"Want me to help you with the gown, madam?"

"No, I've got to go out first." Pulling her jeans back on and donning a sweatshirt, she said, "I'll be back within the hour to prepare for the event tonight. Make sure you're here to help me."

Sofia heard the car engine start up. She heaved a sigh of relief. Thank goodness for the phone call. She'd been sure that she'd get the sharp end of Lauren's temper and a beating to go with it.

She sat on the bed and surveyed the mess. Make-up littered every surface and all the drawers and cupboards had been left open. She'd just begun the thankless task of putting everything straight when she spotted Lauren's mistake.

And what a mistake! Perhaps the biggest blunder the villain's wife had ever made, and one which might offer Sofia the freedom she craved.

Lauren had unlocked the safe to take out the sapphires but, in her haste to leave, had left it open. The door stood wide, temptation staring Sofia in the face. She peered in, curiously. The safe was stacked high with jewellery boxes. She reached out to touch one and pulled her arm back as if it had burned her. This was silly. Lauren was gone, Jacob was out too, no one would see if she just had a peek.

The box contained a necklace of glistening rubies. Stunned by their flawless beauty, Sofia gazed at the way they caught the light.

Had it been one of the many presents Jacob had bought his wife? Perhaps he had been making up for one of his many transgressions. Sofia debated with herself. Should she keep them? Trouble was, she knew nothing about jewellery or how to convert it into hard cash and get a good deal. And it was cash she needed.

Sofia was putting the box back, when on the bottom shelf she spotted a package wrapped in plastic. A quick peek and she knew immediately what it was — heroin. Unlike the necklace, this was a commodity she did know how to trade. She put the package, along with another wrapped just like it, and a black velvet bag into the pocket of her apron. Such an opportunity would not come again.

Sofia had no idea what the heroin was worth but she knew people who did, and they would give her a fair price. Her stomach was turning somersaults. She might even be in possession of enough money to start again but, however much they raised, the packages were her ticket out of here.

CHAPTER TWO

Monday

"Who found her?" DCI Rachel King asked.

DS Elwyn Pryce nodded towards a pew at the far end of the church. "Dorothea Hart, that woman over there."

"Did she see or hear anything?"

"No, the victim's been dead since after the last service last night. Mrs Hart came in this morning. She's had quite a fright and is about to be whisked off to hospital for a check-up. She's been having heart palpitations since finding her friend like that."

Rachel nodded. "Poor woman. Not the best start to a Monday morning."

It wasn't for her either. Rachel was a bag of nerves. She took a deep breath, hoping it would steady her. She was out of practice, an alien in an environment that she should be perfectly familiar with — namely, a murder scene. Was she being too hard on herself? Possibly. After all, she'd spent the last three months idling on the North Wales coast, effectively in witness protection. Only now did she realise what this time away from her demanding job had done. It was as if she had forgotten all her years of training and experience. First day back and she was plunged headlong into this horror and was seriously doubting her ability to cope. For several seconds, she remained tongue-tied, not knowing what to ask. "Has Mrs Hart given you anything useful?" It sounded lame.

"She told me that it was the victim's turn to come in and clean-up after the Sunday services," Elwyn replied. "Mary Dunn would have come back here alone after the evening service to see to the flowers for today. Apparently, she had something of a talent in that department. That would see her here at about eight. Dr Butterworth reckons she's been here all night, so that fits."

That was something at least. "Mrs Hart must have got a real shock. It's a horrific thing to find." Rachel swallowed hard and took another look at the body. The elderly woman had gaffer tape over her mouth. Her hands were crossed over her chest, tied with white ribbon in a bow. A single white rose had been placed between her fingers.

She turned her face away. "What d'you make of it?"

Elwyn shook his head. "I've no idea. It's certainly odd. I've never seen anything like it before."

Rachel turned to Dr Colin Butterworth, the Home Office pathologist. He and Dr Jude Glover, the senior forensic scientist, were examining the body and its surroundings.

"There are no obvious injuries other than the stab wound in her back," Butterworth said. "I'd say the blade was long and sharp. It's difficult to see the wound the way she's lying, but I'll be able to give you more on that once I get her to the lab. There don't appear to be any defensive wounds. It's possible that he came at her from behind, taking her unawares. One quick movement, the blade goes in between the ribs and possibly into the heart, and that's the end of it. Death would have been quick."

Rachel cleared her throat. "What then? He picks her up and places her on the altar?"

"It looks that way. The kill site is over there." He pointed. "You can see the pool of blood on the floor."

"You reckon we're looking for a man then?"

Butterworth thought about this for a moment. "She's a small woman and slight, so the killer could have been female. Of course, it would help to know if it was premeditated or not. When women kill, Rachel, it tends to be more in the heat of the moment."

Rachel breathed easier, she was getting into her stride, asking questions. This is what she did, she reminded herself, and had been doing for many years. Before her enforced break, dealing with such cases had been second nature to her. Now her confidence was gradually flowing back. She took a few steps towards the altar for a closer look. Mary Dunn looked peaceful, but her spirit must be raging at the wickedness of the act.

"Can the body be moved?" Rachel asked.

Butterworth nodded, and gave her a smile. "Good to have you back, Rachel. You were missed."

"Indeed, you were," Jude agreed. "I know we had the odd chat on the phone but it's not the same, is it? Girls okay?"

Rachel grimaced. How to answer that one? "Mixed. Mia's fine, she's picked up exactly where she left off, but Megan's being cagey about going back to uni. That one worries me to death. She's got her first year under her belt and told me she loved the course. I don't understand her."

"Has she got an alternative in mind?"

"She wants to go travelling with a mate. I'm terrified at the thought — Megan out there in the big wide world, anything could happen."

"And what about the baby? How's little Len doing?"

The mention of Len's name brought a smile to Rachel's face. "He's more toddler now than baby and growing like it's going out of fashion. Bawls his head off at the least thing — basically a right handful." She grinned. "Which reminds me, I'll have to sort something permanent on the childcare front. I've left him with Alan and Belinda today but that's not ideal. That was supposed to be my first job this morning, sussing out the nurseries."

"Given that Alan's not Len's dad, I tend to agree," Jude said. "Though he's always supported you with the kids."

9

"Can't take advantage though. It wouldn't be fair."

"Dare I ask if you've heard from Jed?"

At the sound of his name, Rachel's stomach did a little somersault. She shook her head. "And I don't want to, Jude. Me and Jed McAteer are well and truly over."

Did she really mean that? During the last three months, Rachel had been on something of an emotional rollercoaster on the Jed front. She had no idea how she'd react should he suddenly walk back into her life. The thought terrified her. Throughout their relationship they'd had good times and bad. The best thing to come out of the recent resurgence of her romance with him was their son, Len. He was too young to ask questions but there would come a time when that would change. Wondering what she'd tell him then kept her awake at nights.

Jed had been the love of her life since they were at college together. Then their paths diverged — Rachel joined the police, and in stark contrast, Jed became one of Manchester's most notorious villains. In the last few years he'd redeemed himself, he'd made a new start and wanted Rachel back in his life. All was going well for the pair and to top things off, little Len came along. He was only weeks old when it all blew up. Jed reverted to type, got involved with a gang of dangerous villains and put Rachel and the children in grave danger. Rachel could not forgive him for that and had to finally come to terms with the fact that the long-standing romance was over for good.

CHAPTER THREE

While Rachel and the doctors were talking, Elwyn had been asking Dorothea Hart about the victim. Once the paramedic had wheeled her away to the waiting ambulance, he joined Rachel. "Mary Dunn was a regular member of the congregation here," he told her. "A dozen or so of the women take it in turns to keep the church in order. There's a rota, apparently, but Mary always did the flowers. I'll see if the vicar has a copy we can have. We need to work out if Mary was the intended target, or if the killer wasn't fussy who he found in the church and she was simply unlucky."

"It's too soon to say anything," Rachel decided. "We need to find out a great deal more about the people she knew and her recent past. We'll speak to her family, her friends, and see what they have to say."

"Mrs Hart tells me that Mary has a daughter living close by," Elwyn said. "We'll speak to her, of course, but we should have a look at Mary's home too. Hopefully, the daughter will have a key to her mother's place. But first the vicar. Let's see what he can tell us."

Rachel nodded. Thank goodness for Elwyn. The mention of Jed McAteer had distracted her and her mind had gone blank again. "Where do we find this vicar?"

11

"Reverend Henry Neville lives in the cottage behind the church," Elwyn said.

"Come on then, let's go and have a word."

Elwyn led the way, out of the rear door, along a cobbled path to the vicar's stone cottage. The garden was beautifully tended, with a colourful array of flowers surrounding a small lawn. Looking at the building and the land around it you'd never know you were only a stone's throw from the city centre.

"I had a quick word with him earlier," Elwyn said. "The building has been here two centuries, so he told me. You could walk around this area of town all day, marvel at the number of new-builds, the high-rise apartments going up, and completely miss this."

Rachel trailed her hand over the wisteria hanging from the cottage porch. "It's some garden he's got, too. This is a regular oasis."

The man who answered Elwyn's knock was in his sixties, tall with short, greying hair and what Rachel thought of as a fixed smile. The word that sprang instantly to mind was *insincere* and it bothered her — she'd not even spoken to him yet.

"You're here about poor Mary," Reverend Henry Neville said soberly. "Dreadful thing to happen. She certainly didn't deserve that. We shall all miss her."

His little spiel sounded well practised, spoken in a monotone, obviously brought out whenever he had to comfort the recently bereaved. Rachel examined his face for any trace of genuine emotion. She saw none. For a man of God there was a lot of darkness in his eyes.

Rachel had no idea why she should react this way. Why these feelings about a complete stranger? Could she trust them? Maybe it was to do with her long absence from the job. It was something to be discussed with Elwyn later. She shook herself. This man was a vicar, not a suspect.

"Have any members of the congregation been threatened recently?" she asked. "For instance, did you hear anyone mention being afraid, or seeing strangers hanging around the churchyard?"

Neville shook his head. "No, and I'm sure one of the ladies would have said something if that was the case. We have good community policing round here. I encourage all members of my congregation to report anything illegal they become aware of."

"What about Mary? Did she seem worried about anything?" Elwyn asked.

"I think her grandson, Ronan, might have been giving her grief. He's her daughter Kimberley's lad. I've seen him several times recently, lurking in the graveyard. A few nights ago, he was definitely up to something. I don't know a great deal about the subject, the details and the like, but I think he was dealing drugs."

"Why would you think that?" Elwyn asked.

"I know there's a lot of it goes on around here and for such a young lad, Ronan never seems to be short of money. I have my younger brother, George, staying with me currently. The pair of us were litter picking in the churchyard about dusk a couple of nights ago. We heard voices, and watched the proceedings for a while from behind the large oak. Ronan set himself up just inside the main gate and for the next thirty minutes there was a procession of youngsters coming and going. I couldn't see exactly what was changing hands, but money was definitely involved. One of the youngsters was handing something over to young Ronan but dropped it on the path. It was a roll of banknotes. George straightaway cottoned on that it was drug dealing. Mark my words, that grandson of hers is a bad 'un."

"Didn't you approach them?" Elwyn asked.

"George is younger than me but even so, we're both getting on in years. We didn't dare." He looked a little sheepish. "There are lads round here who'd slit your throat soon as look at you. Ronan's a no-hoper. I'm sorry if that sounds harsh but it's the truth. He's bad to the core."

Rachel made no comment. She'd reserve judgement until she'd met the lad and knew more about his background.

"Does it go on a lot, the dealing?" Elwyn asked.

"I've not seen it before but then I don't go looking for it. I told our community police officer, who said he'd have a word with Ronan and keep an eye out. There was little else he could do, since we had no real proof."

"Did you tell Mary?" Rachel asked.

"No. I considered it but decided it would have been the wrong thing to do. Mary did so much for the church and I knew that if she discovered the truth — that Ronan had been using the premises to ply his evil trade — she'd stop coming." The vicar shook his head. "Apart from that, how could I explain to Mary just how bad her grandson was? She knew Ronan was no angel, but if she found out that he was possibly a drug dealer, even small-time, it would have finished her. She doted on him."

"It could be what got her killed," Elwyn pointed out. He handed the vicar a card. "Next time you witness anything similar, don't bother with the community police, just give us a ring."

"D'you have a copy of the rota for cleaning the church?" Rachel asked.

The vicar took a sheet of paper from the hall table. "Here. Mary drew it up every month. This is the latest version."

"Is there ever any trouble in the church? You know, vandalism, thefts, that sort of thing?" Rachel asked.

"No. There used to be but nowadays all the church silver is kept locked in a bank vault. We have nothing there worth stealing. Even the charity box is securely fastened down."

CHAPTER FOUR

"What did you think of the vicar?" Rachel asked as they walked towards Elwyn's car.

"He's a man of God, they're usually the good sort, aren't they, or have I got that wrong?"

"It's just that I got this feeling. There's something not right about him, but I've no idea what." She pulled a face. "But perhaps it's me that's got it wrong. I've been away a while, Elwyn, I'm out of practice."

He smiled. "Your copper's instinct needs time to settle, to sharpen up, that's all it is."

Rachel hoped he was right and that she'd soon get back to normal. "Where does the daughter live?"

"Less than five minutes away. We'll go in yours and I'll pick my car up on the way back. It's a cul-de-sac at the end of Locksey Street."

"Okay." Rachel glanced his way, a grin on her face. "Are you going to tell me about it, or do I have to make do with the gossip?"

He grinned back ruefully. "I intended to tell you this morning, really I did, but then we got the shout about the murder. To be honest, I find it all a bit embarrassing. It'll take some getting used to. Suddenly I'm a man of means.

15

I've got a bank account stuffed with money I didn't have to slog my guts out for and it scares me to death. What am I supposed to do with it? I've got a house, a job I love and there's nothing I need."

Rachel laughed. "Poor you. Your gran wanted you and your sister to enjoy yourselves with it, so do just that. How is your mum? She must be upset at losing her."

"My mother is a realist. Gran was old and she was ill. Mum and Dad don't need the money — they're okay and Gran knew that. Apart from Mum, Gran only had me and Ffion."

"Well, lucky you, that's what I say. Next time you have some leave, take a holiday somewhere exotic, see a bit of the world."

Elwyn smiled but said nothing. Rachel took that to mean it was already on his list. He turned off the main road and pulled into the cul-de-sac. "She knows we're coming, though not why."

"Poor woman, to lose your mum like that and with the possibility that it had something to do with your son. This won't be pleasant." In the last three months, Rachel had forgotten about the misery factor. How the unexpected presence of the police in people's lives usually meant news of the worst sort. She got out of Elwyn's car with a familiar feeling of dread.

"You okay?" Elwyn asked. "Only you've gone a tad pale. Sure you haven't come back a bit too soon?"

The truth was, Rachel was finding it hard going. She needed to get a grip, sort out her head, and quick. "I'm all over the place. It was seeing the body like that. As for coming back too soon, Elwyn, I don't think the time will ever be right. After what happened with Jed, I'm worried I might have lost it. For the first time ever, the job is making me anxious. I'm afraid of the villains, of not being there for the kids, but most of all, I'm scared of getting it wrong."

Elwyn wasn't having that. "You're a good detective, Rachel, we all know that, and if you're honest with yourself so do you. Look at the complex cases you've solved over the years, the villains you've put away."

But Rachel wasn't convinced. "We'll see. We do well with this one and I'll have another think. But I'm not promising anything."

"You know I've always got your back."

How right he was. The soft-spoken Welshman had been a true friend throughout. "I'm eternally grateful to you, Elwyn, and not just on the professional front. Allowing me and the kids to stay in your parents' bungalow saved the day. I had nowhere to go."

"Witness protection would have sorted you out."

"Yes, but living by the sea like that for a few months in a quiet town, it was nice. It took me out of myself, and the kids had a good time too. I even made the odd friend, had a couple of nights out."

He grinned. "Sounds interesting. Anyone in particular?"

She smiled. "Might be. And that's all I'm saying."

Elwyn allowed her reply to slide. He pulled up outside the house. "Here we go, and don't worry, you'll be fine. The daughter's name is Kimberley Dunn, by the way. She's thirty-eight, unmarried but in a relationship and works at the soap-packing works round the corner."

Potted history over, the pair made their way to the front door.

The woman who answered was a hard-faced brassy blonde, plastered in make-up. She looked them up and down. "If this is about our Ronan, you're wasting my time and yours. I've 'ad it with the lad. I'm sick of telling him 'cause no way does he ever listen."

"This is about your mum," Elwyn said kindly, showing her his badge. "I'm DS Elwyn Pryce and this is Detective Chief Inspector King."

Her eyes, heavy with mascara, flicked from one of them to the other. "My mum? What's happened? What's she done?" As she spoke, Kimberley Dunn was checking her mobile. "Can't be much. This time in the morning she'll be at the community centre down the road, it's bingo today."

"I'm afraid your mum's dead, Kimberley," Rachel told her. "She was found in the church earlier today. She'd been murdered."

The dark eyes blinked, and Kimberley Dunn keeled over. Elwyn caught her a split second before she hit the floor. He helped her to a chair in the hallway. "Get some water, Rachel."

"She can't be dead," Kimberley muttered. "Who'd want to kill my mum? She's a gem. There's no one else like her."

Rachel handed her a glass of water. "Sip on this. That's right. Kimberley, we're going to need your help. We've got questions and, painful as they will be, we're hoping you have some of the answers."

"I don't know anyone who'd wish her harm, if that's what you mean," Kimberley said. "Everyone she met loved her — ask that vicar."

"We've spoken to him, but he has limited information. We need to know more about the family and the people she knew. Did she owe anyone money for instance? Had she made any enemies?"

Kimberley frowned. "I'm trying to think. Her friends are all like her. They go to the church, the community centre and bingo once a week. She's not met anyone new in ages — well, apart from my boyfriend, Jack Fairhurst, and he's harmless enough."

"What does he do, this Mr Fairhurst?" Elwyn asked.

Kimberley stuck her nose in the air. "He's between jobs at the moment but he'll find something. It's only a matter of time. Don't go thinking he had anything to do with it. He thought my mum was lovely."

"Where does he live?"

"Sometimes here with me, sometimes in Longsight with his brother."

"We've been told your son might be involved in drug dealing. Your mum's death could possibly be connected to that," Rachel said.

Kimberley's head jerked up. She looked hard at Rachel. "Ronan? Why would you think that? He loves his gran. Anyway, he'd never hurt a pensioner, that's not his thing at all."

"Perhaps not, but what about the people he deals with? They could be leaning on Ronan, getting at him through his family," Elwyn suggested.

"Look, the only lad he goes on about who has anything to do with drugs is Arlo. But it won't have anything to do with him. Too fond of keeping out of the limelight is Arlo."

"Does Arlo have a full name?" Rachel asked.

"No idea, love. Everyone round 'ere just knows him as Arlo. Makes out he's the main man when it comes to drugs."

"Does Ronan owe him money?" Elwyn asked.

Kimberley Dunn shrugged. "He could do. He's a piece of work, my son. No morals and only out for himself, but he'd never do a murder, and certainly not his gran. Not got the balls apart from anything else."

"When's he usually at home?" Elwyn asked.

"No idea. I haven't seen him these last three weeks. He'll be staying with a mate."

"Which one, and where?"

"Look, Ronan's seventeen, he's a big lad with a life of his own. I don't interfere and that's how we both like it."

"Okay, Kimberley, but you can get in touch with him, can't you?" Rachel said.

Kimberley nodded.

"Ring him. Tell him what's happened and that we want to speak to him. You can give us his number too."

"He won't like it. Does his best to avoid the police, does Ronan."

Rachel bent over the still sobbing woman and brought her face close to hers. "Trust me, we find him first, have to drag him in, and the experience won't be pleasant. We'll assume he's got something to hide and dig into every corner of his grubby little life."

She might be upset about her mother, but Kimberley's attitude annoyed Rachel. Why the refusal to help?

Kimberley sniffed. "I'll try his mobile, though when he sees it's me, he won't answer."

"Send him a text," Rachel snapped back. "We'll need to search your mother's home too. I'll need her address and the key."

From a shelf by the door, Kimberley took down a key on a length of string. "The block of pensioners' flats, up the street. The low-rise ones, two storey, you can't miss 'em. She lived at number ten."

"Thank you," Rachel said, pocketing the key. "If we need to take anything away, we'll make sure you get it back. You ring Ronan and make sure he knows the score. Tell him if he doesn't report to the police within twenty-four hours then I'll put a call out for his arrest and that of this Arlo person too. Word will soon get round that all the police interest is down to your son. What chance his safety on the street then?"

"You're a right bitch, d'you know that?" Kimberley said.

Rachel might be out of practice but the old taunts were still water off a duck's back. If the job was going to work at all, it was time to toughen up.

CHAPTER FIVE

The pair learned from the caretaker that Mary's flat was on the ground floor at the rear of the building, one of those with a view out over the large communal garden. He let them in through the main doors and led them along a corridor to her door.

"It's unlocked," Rachel said. "Is that usual?"

The caretaker scratched his head. "No, she was a stickler for security. Perhaps she left in a hurry."

But Rachel didn't think so. "You need to know the code to gain entrance through the main doors, don't you?"

He nodded.

"Okay, thanks."

"What're you thinking?" Elwyn asked as soon as he'd gone.

"One of the other residents could have wanted a look round, or someone could have got in as another person left. Are there any cameras?" she asked.

"No. I took a look as we came in."

Rachel donned a pair of nitrile gloves and examined the lock. It looked okay, hadn't been tampered with. "Ask Butterworth to check if Mary had the key on her."

"Perhaps it's as the caretaker said and Mary left in a rush," Elwyn said.

"Perhaps," Rachel replied. "But we'll keep our minds open. Get Forensics to dust the place for prints."

She stood in the sitting room, gazing out through the large picture window. The garden was well tended with flower beds and a raised vegetable plot at the far end.

"Everything looks as it should," Elwyn said, coming up to join her. "The kitchen's next door and the one bedroom and bathroom are off the hallway. Apart from her being a bit of a hoarder there's nothing out of place, no ransacked drawers or cupboards."

"Fair enough. Despite the front door then, it doesn't look as if anyone's been here. That's something, I suppose." She turned to him. "When you say hoarder, what d'you mean?"

He smiled. "The piles of old newspapers in the hall and under the sink. My gran was just the same."

"Odd ideas the elderly have about throwing stuff away."

"Given that we reckon it wasn't down to robbery, what are we looking for?" Elwyn asked.

"I've no idea. Something that points to what got her killed. Currently her grandson and his drug-dealing mates are top of the list." Rachel scanned the room. There was nothing there of any obvious value. The odd antique vase that might fetch a bob or two and a silver-framed photo of a boy Rachel took to be Ronan, aged about seven. "You've put out the call for Ronan and this new 'main man', Arlo?"

"I've got Amy on it," Elwyn said.

Rachel looked at the innocent face of the youngster in the photo. For the first time in a long while her instinct was piqued. It told her it wasn't Ronan. But who then? What was it about Mary Dunn that had got her so brutally murdered?

"She's had her old photos out too." Elwyn picked up one of the albums off the sideboard. "I wonder what she was looking for? Some of the snaps in here are ancient."

Rachel smiled. "Old black and white ones. I can't see them having any relevance to her murder, but you never know."

"There's three albums and a chocolate box full. Want to take them with us?"

Would they help? "Okay, but it's probably a waste of time. I bet she was simply reminiscing about the past with her old friends."

The pair heard a knock at the door. Elwyn answered to find an elderly man on the doorstep. He looked distraught.

"It's not true, is it? Please tell me there's been some dreadful mistake. Mary was a key member of our little community here. I can't imagine the place without her."

"And you are?"

"Reg Hitchin. I live next door. I helped Mary tend the garden. She was a wonder. Most years she grew enough vegetables to feed the lot of us through the winter."

"I'm afraid Mary has been killed," Elwyn told him gently. "We're detectives, trying to find out what happened. We're speaking to her family and her friends."

Reg Hitchin started to shake. "It's the shock. I'll have to sit for a moment." He carefully lowered himself onto the sofa. "Killed, you say, that's terrible. Poor Mary. We're all her friends here and will be only too happy to help you."

"Mr Hitchin, are you aware if Mary had been upset by anyone recently?" he asked.

Wiping a tear from his cheek, Reg shook his head. "No. Everyone who knew Mary loved her, she was a wonderful woman. It was her who got everyone organised, told us all what to do in the garden. We even had an open day last year. It raised some cash for seeds and the like. Without her it would never have been as successful as it was."

"Living next door, were you aware of any visitors?" Rachel asked him. "Particularly during the last couple of days."

"Only Kim, her daughter, and Dotty, of course. That's her best friend, Dorothea. Mary and Dotty helped out at the church. Her last visitors were Kim, who was here Saturday and Dotty, who called for her before the service on Sunday morning."

"No one else? You're sure of that?"

"No. The weather's been nice recently. Mary had been spending most of her time working in the garden with the rest of us."

"D'you know her grandson, Ronan?" Rachel asked.

"Indeed, I do. Now there's one young lad who needs taking in hand. Runs wild and has no respect, but I haven't seen him here recently."

"You're sure?" Rachel insisted. "Only it could be important."

"His mother banned him from visiting Mary a few months ago. But I've seen him in the park, bothering the kids and that. Mary, I know, hoped he'd grow out of his wicked ways. She loved that lad, had doted on him ever since he was an infant. The fact that he wasn't allowed to visit upset her, but Kim thought it best."

"Why was he banned?" Rachel asked.

Reg gave a deep sigh. "He was stealing things from her. Small items, silver, pottery figures and the like. Stuff he could get a few bob for at the market. Mary never noticed but Kim did."

"Mary and Dorothea — they were good friends, were they?"

Reg nodded. "Ever since their schooldays. Poor Dotty will be gutted. Have you spoken to her?"

"Not yet. She's in hospital being checked over. She found Mary and the shock made her unwell. Once she's feeling better, we'll have a chat."

Reg gave Rachel a puzzled look. He seemed to want to ask her more about the murder but didn't dare. Maybe he was too afraid of what Rachel would tell him. She was grateful for that. How to describe to this frail, elderly man what Mary's oldest friend had seen when she'd entered the church this morning?

CHAPTER SIX

When Rachel walked into the main office, a loud cheer went up.

"Welcome back, ma'am," Detective Jonny Farrell said, all smiles. "The place hasn't been the same without you."

Detective Constable Amy Metcalfe gave a small nod. She and Rachel had had their differences in the past, and it was obvious that Amy wasn't quite so pleased to see her as the others.

"It's good to see you lot too. I've missed you all, the job, this place, and it's great to finally be at work again. Although a day or so sitting at my desk getting used to the idea would have been good." Slipping off her coat, Rachel looked at Amy. "Ronan Dunn, our victim's grandson, see if anything's known. Also, a drug dealer known on the streets as 'Arlo'."

Rachel's office looked spick and span and there were fresh flowers in a vase on the windowsill. Elwyn, she guessed. Her desk was the tidiest she'd ever seen it, and there wasn't a ring from a coffee mug to be seen. She smiled to herself. Nice, but not guaranteed to last long, not the way she worked.

Back in the main office, Elwyn was at the incident board, writing down what little they had. "Our victim is one Mary Dunn, eighty-four years old," he told the others. "The woman appears to have led a blameless life. Last night she was stabbed to death in her local church and left on the altar, mouth taped up, hands tied in white ribbon and crossed over her chest. She also had a white rose between her fingers."

Rachel noticed Amy wince.

"That's weird," Jonny said. "Rather distinctive."

"Is her grandson, this Ronan, a suspect?" Jonny asked.

"Currently he's the only lead we've got," Rachel said, joining Elwyn at the board. "The vicar suspects he was dealing drugs and getting them off this Arlo character. We need a word, find out what the pair of them were doing on Sunday night. One theory is that Mary discovered that her grandson was using the churchyard to ply his trade, came down hard on him and this Arlo character stepped in. Maybe the pair of them decided it would teach the locals a lesson, show them what happens to those who interfere."

While Rachel was speaking, Amy had been doing a little research. "Arlo is known to the drug squad, ma'am. They've hauled him in a couple of times. Nothing found on him though, so they couldn't charge him."

Far too clever to be caught with the gear on him. He'd have a mate with him for that. "No chance of an address, I suppose?" Rachel asked.

"When he was brought in the last time, his address was Bright House, Ancoats. It's one of the new apartment blocks."

Rachel looked at Elwyn. "Right then, let's go and have a word." She looked round the room at the expectant faces. "Ronan Dunn should check in. When he does, keep him here."

"Rachel. A word."

Superintendent Mark Kenton had come into the office and had been listening from the back of the room. "I'd like a quick chat in my office."

With a quick backward grimace at Elwyn, she followed Kenton out. "Sorry I've not had time to bring you up to date. I'm back and straight into a murder case."

Once in his office and with the door firmly shut, Kenton said, "These two characters you're looking for, Ronan and Arlo. Drop it."

Rachel was taken aback. No pleasantries, no welcome back, he'd simply barked the order at her. "I can't, sir. They could both be instrumental in finding out who killed Mary Dunn."

"If you get further evidence that they are, then we'll interview them, but for now leave the pair to the drug squad." Kenton shrugged. "Not ideal but I've had my orders. That Arlo in particular is known to them and is being closely watched. You wade in and question him, and he'll run. The squad could lose him for good."

"That's a shame. I wanted to question him about Ronan Dunn. Find out what the pair were doing over the weekend."

"On Saturday afternoon, Arlo, Ronan and two others went to Holyhead. They picked up three packing crates from the docks, one of which contained a large amount of cocaine. It was a sting. The drug squad were waiting. They wanted to get their hands on the people shipping the stuff across. It was successful and the squad are pleased with the outcome. Ronan, plus his cohorts, spent the whole weekend languishing in a North Wales jail while the Welsh police checked things out, so neither he nor Arlo Bain could have harmed Mary Dunn."

That was something at least, but it didn't help her case. "And Arlo, what about him? He's older and a known associate of Ronan's."

"Arlo is also a member of a gang run by one Jacob Gilbert, a man the drug squad are desperate to get evidence on. Like I said, Rachel, get the evidence and we'll bring him in, but until then Arlo's out of bounds to us."

"What about Gilbert?"

"Look him up," Kenton said. "But be aware, he's not someone you want to tangle with. Particularly not after your recent experience with Hutton and Blackmore."

Rachel gave an involuntary shudder. "Their shoes haven't remained empty for long then."

"Word has it they've been filled by Gilbert, a one-time member of Hutton's gang, so he knows the ropes and the names of those who are only too willing to help him."

Manchester's gangland. The mere thought gave Rachel the shivers. Grace Blackmore in particular had been the reason behind her 'holiday' in North Wales. Grace had made credible threats to kill both her and her family.

Time to get a grip. "Are Bain and Ronan due to be released on bail?"

"Yes, and when they are, they'll be brought back here for questioning by the drug squad."

"Amy has checked for Ronan Dunn on the system, but his name didn't come up."

"Ronan is his street name. His real name is Ronald Hampton. His mother didn't marry his father but gave him the name anyway."

Kimberley should have told them that. "Ronald's not cool enough for the underworld in the eyes of a seventeen-year-old boy."

"Whatever the reason, it doesn't help us find Mary's killer." Kenton was growing impatient. "There has to be something else. You'll have to dig a bit deeper, Rachel. Mary Dunn must have upset someone, or been the victim of some scam and become a liability. Think of where she lives — Ancoats has its fair share of villains."

"Has its fair share of wealthy business types these days too. Isn't that a bit far-fetched, sir? The woman was eighty-four years old and a pillar of her community. So far not a single person has had a bad word to say about her. Her flat is spotless and, despite an unlocked door, there's no obvious sign of a break-in. The neighbours haven't seen anyone odd hanging about." She sighed and shook her head. "She's the last person anyone would want to murder, it's as simple as that. And then we discover that her grandson has been dealing drugs and is known to a dealer in hock to a dangerous gangster. You can see where I'm going, can't you?"

"It's the wrong avenue of enquiry," Kenton insisted. "Have you considered that the killer chose his victim at random or simply got the wrong woman?"

This was not something that had occurred to her and, in her opinion, it was highly unlikely. But should she give it credibility? This was silly. She was a DCI not a novice. "We'll investigate. But what's the betting we'll find no suspects among her friends or neighbours?"

Kenton shook his head dismissively. "There has to be something, even the random element. Keep me in the loop, Rachel. It's good to have you back, by the way," he said at last. "Don't overdo it, utilise your team. It'll do them no harm to take up the slack."

Try telling Amy that, she thought.

"Where're you living by the way?"

"At home, the house I've lived in for years."

"It's one of two semi-detached cottages isn't it?"

"It was, but Jed bought the one next door from Alan and knocked them into one large cottage. One of the last decent things Jed did was to sign the place over to me. I own the lot outright." She smiled. "Mind you, I'm not sure if I'll stay there. Too many ghosts."

"Worth a packet though, given where it is, in deepest Cheshire."

He was right but Rachel hadn't given it much thought. Perhaps she should. The money the house would bring would give her and the kids a completely new start.

CHAPTER SEVEN

Rachel returned to the main office where the team were hard at it, heads down, no doubt trying to find out where Ronan was hiding. She'd have to put a stop to that. "Forget Ronan Dunn for now. Arlo too. Whatever this is about, Kenton is sure it has nothing to do with them."

She saw the quizzical looks but couldn't tell them what she knew. The more people who knew that the drug squad were on to the two of them, the more danger of leaks.

"Has the Super said something then?" Jonny asked. "Does he know this Arlo character?"

Rachel spread her hands. "You'll just have to trust me. For now, we drop our investigations into him and Ronan. Kenton's given me information which proves that whoever murdered Mary, it wasn't that pair."

"Jude's been on," Elwyn said. "She's asked if we'll go and see her."

Rachel nodded, grateful for the change of tack. With luck, Jude had something for them, possibly the lead they so badly needed. "While we're gone, the rest of you find out all you can about Mary, her friends and her daughter, Kimberley. Also, that creepy vicar, Henry Neville. He was quick to point the finger at young Ronan, which could mean he has something to hide."

Well, it might, but what? What dark secrets could a vicar possibly have? All in all, Mary's friends and family were a mild bunch — with the possible exception of Kimberley.

"Clutching at straws, Rachel?" Elwyn said as they headed out. "The vicar did it — is that what we're going for now? Sounds like some detective novel."

"No, of course not, but we know nothing about him. He made my hackles rise when I first saw him, so it'll do no harm. We need a full picture after all."

"Has Kenton warned you off Arlo and Ronan? Hope he gave you an explanation."

"They are of interest to the drug squad. They're hoping to catch the pair red-handed in some deal or other. Ronan was held in a prison on Anglesey all weekend, so he couldn't have killed his gran. Kenton is concerned that our involvement will blow it for the squad, hence we back off."

"This Arlo character is well known. He's been brought in before, spent the odd night in the cells here, in fact," Elwyn said.

"Kenton suggested we look at Mary being the wrong target, the possibility that the killer made a mistake. Or that she was simply a random killing."

"It is a possibility, I suppose, but I doubt it's that simple," Elwyn said.

"Me too. She was too well known in the community."

They arrived at the morgue to find Jude waiting for them in the lab. "Colin has done the post-mortem and found he'd been wrong. Mary did put up a fight — well, a bit of one anyway. We think the killer went for her from behind. The knife went in between the ribs and entered the heart. When the attack began, she must have reached back and grabbed at his hair, which was quite long. She pulled some hairs out, which we found on her coat collar."

"You're sure it's not hers?"

"No, the hair I found on her collar is grey, coarse. Mary's is fine and white." Jude gave them a big smile. "Some of it has the root still attached, so I should get a DNA match."

"Brilliant. Now we just have to hope he's on the database," Elwyn said.

"Even if he isn't, this information is a help. We know we're looking for someone with grey hair. At the very least, we know to look for someone older."

"I intend to rush this through, and I'll be in touch," Jude promised.

"Is there anything else of interest?" Rachel asked.

"When she was attacked, Mary had been doing the flowers — getting rid of the dead ones, changing the water, that sort of thing. My team had a good look round inside the church, and there were no white roses in any of the vases. It made me wonder where the killer got the rose he placed on her body. It's occurred to me since that he might have picked it up from outside, taken it from one of the graves," Jude said.

"He could have brought it with him," Elwyn said.

"A lot of trouble to go to when there's plenty of other flowers around," Rachel added.

"Perhaps the white rose has some special significance," Jude suggested. "It struck me that you might want to look at your database and see if it and the ribbon have featured before."

Rachel nudged Elwyn. "We'll have another look at the church ourselves before we call it a day." She gave Jude a smile. "Did Colin find anything else of interest?"

"We'll have to wait until the results of the tests are in. Like I said before, it would've been quick," Jude said.

Rachel straightened up. "Right. A scout round the churchyard and then we'll get off home."

"What are we expecting to find?" Elwyn asked.

"White roses," Rachel said. "And then I thought we'd have another word with the vicar. I've got a couple more questions for him. For a start, I'd like to know why he was so keen to implicate Ronan."

"Trying to get the lad off the streets and out of his hair, no doubt," Elwyn said.

But Rachel wasn't so sure.

* * *

The graveyard was old and no longer in use. Most of the headstones were crumbling or fallen over, the graves long since left untended. But in a corner to the right of the church entrance, the graves were more recent, dating from the last twenty years or so. A few of these bore flowers or plants.

The two detectives, followed at a distance by the vicar, walked between the graves, looking for any with white roses.

"Oh look. Albert Dunn," Elwyn called out. "Says here 'beloved husband of Mary'."

"Any flowers?" Rachel asked.

"No, but there's water in the vase and white petals on the grass. It looks suspiciously like someone's made off with whatever flowers were here."

Rachel went to where Elwyn was bent over examining the grave site. She picked up a few petals. "They're rose petals, all right. White ones too. We need Forensics here. They didn't search the graveyard. I suspect the killer took the rose from here, kept it to place on Mary's body and disposed of the rest."

This might give them the lead they needed. Rachel noticed boot prints in the mud beside the grave. She walked on, looking at the other recent graves. One, in particular, caught her eye, the grave of a Katie Neville. She called back to the vicar, "A relative of yours?" Rachel looked more closely at the inscription on the headstone and saw that the girl was only sixteen years old when she died.

"A distant relative. A very sad case, she died far too young," the vicar said. Rachel waited for him to continue but instead he nodded at the grave they had been looking at. "Mary's husband. Useful chap in his day. Did a lot of repair work for the church."

"Kindly stay back," Rachel said. "We may have found something. Did Mary regularly put flowers on his grave?"

"Most weeks. She liked to see it looking nice."

"We'll have to tape this area off, get our people here to look at it," Rachel told him.

"As you wish," the vicar said. "Have you found young Ronan yet?"

"Yes, and he's not involved, he's got an alibi," Rachel said. "Why were you so keen for us to go after him?"

"The dealing, no other reason. I was worried that if he carried on, he'd end up in trouble." The reverend gave her that fixed smile.

"You don't like him much, do you?" Rachel said bluntly.

The smile disappeared. "I'm not proud of it, but no. I find the lad rude and unpleasant. He's always keen to poke fun at me and what I do."

Rachel could imagine. A fledgling dealer, trying to impress his peers. "Tell me, has anyone new joined your congregation recently?"

The vicar shook his head. "No, and I certainly would have noticed, so would the others. The people who attend my services are a select bunch who've been coming for years. Anyone new would stand out."

While he was talking Rachel's eyes were drawn to the vicar's hair. No way could anyone grab a handful of that, it was far too short. "Okay. Forensics will be here shortly to look at the area around the grave."

"I am sorry I couldn't be more helpful. Mary's murder has upset us all. I, for one, just want the business over with and the killer caught."

"You and me both," Rachel said.

They watched the vicar trudge back to his house.

"I've rung Jude," Elwyn said, "and brought her up to date with what we've found. Back to the station?"

She'd hoped for an early finish on her first day back. No chance of that now. Rachel looked up at the grey sky. It had rained since Mary was throttled to death. "Realistically, what's the chance of getting anything useful from either the vase or around the grave?"

"Jude knows her job," Elwyn said. "If anyone can get forensic evidence from this little lot, it's her."

CHAPTER EIGHT

"I trust you followed your instructions to the letter?"

"Yes, but things can't stay as they are. You have to do something, find somewhere else. The police come looking and I won't be able to protect you."

"You need to be more positive, Henry. I need more time and it's doing no harm. Besides, things go my way and you'll be well rewarded." There was a wicked little laugh.

"You promised that no one would get hurt," Henry Neville spluttered into the phone.

"The old woman was a mistake, she got in the way. Don't worry, she'd have known little about what happened. A quick lunge with the knife and it was over."

Reverend Henry Neville closed his eyes. He had a sudden urge to slam down the phone, but didn't dare — the repercussions didn't bear thinking about. "You're an evil bastard. Poison, that's what you are."

"Don't make me laugh, Henry. You're every bit as evil as me, you just hide it better. That dog collar for starters, it's the perfect disguise until someone bothers to look beyond it. I would hate it to be me who points the way, so you see it's in your interest to help me. There's a new lot running things these days, and you'd be wise not to forget that."

"The police and their forensic teams are all over my church and graveyard. How long d'you think it'll be before they extend their search, eh?"

"In that case, it's up to you to ensure they don't discover our little secret. It should be a simple task in the grand scheme of things. That church of yours is huge and it's rambling. They can search where they like. Cellars and certain other places are easily missed, so it's up to you to make sure that's what happens. I've been careful. I've gone to great pains to ensure there's no evidence to point things my way and plenty to point where I want it."

Henry Neville shook his head. "One of these days you'll come unstuck and everything will point your way. When that finally happens, I want no part of it."

"Do as you're told and your name will be kept out of it."

"If the police do search the church, they'll have a warrant. I can't stop them going wherever they choose."

"Just make sure my secret stays safe, Henry. Find a way. Understand?"

The line went dead. Looking out through his sitting-room window, the reverend saw that they were already setting up their lights in the graveyard. Forensics sent by that interfering woman detective. What would they find? Nothing to cause him any more trouble, he hoped. He had enough on his plate as it was.

* * *

Rachel left Elwyn in the station car park. "Thanks for helping me today," she said. "I hope it doesn't take me too long to get back on form."

"You did just fine," he said.

He was being kind. Rachel was well aware that she was far from being on form. "We'll meet here in the morning and wait for Jude's findings from the graveyard." Watching him make his way back into the station, she called after him. "Don't stay too late."

As Rachel pulled away from the station, she wondered how long she and Elwyn could keep up the pretence. Something had changed. She couldn't put her finger on it, but that elusive quality that had made her a truly good detective had all but deserted her. It was all very well for Elwyn to put it down to the break, but there was more to it than that. During the time she'd spent in the quiet Welsh town, Rachel had found a peace she hadn't experienced in years. She'd found herself loath to give that up.

It took her nearly an hour to reach the country lane in the Cheshire village of Poynton where she lived. She was late. Alan and Belinda must be wondering what had happened to her. No way could she impose on them like this every day, it wasn't fair. It was many years since her and Alan's divorce. Dedicated to the kids he might be, but they weren't Belinda's responsibility. They had their own lives to lead. Still, childcare was a problem. What was she to do with little Len tomorrow for starters.

Her eldest, Megan, met her at the door. "I'm off into town. Don't worry if I'm not back, I'll be at Jason's."

Who the hell is Jason? But Rachel had no time to ask. Already, Megan was at the front gate and climbing into a taxi.

"He works as a programmer for a manufacturing company. She's known him precisely two days but he's already the love of her life."

"Thanks for the update." Rachel smiled, taking Len from Alan's arms. "Mia in?"

"Doing her homework, would you believe."

"If Meg's got herself a boyfriend, she might change her mind about leaving university and travelling," Rachel said.

"We can live in hope." Alan checked the time. "Look, love, I'll have to rush. Belinda's cooking and we're having the neighbours round."

"Sorry about the kids," Rachel said. "I fully intended to be back early, but I've been catapulted into a murder case and it's full on, I'm afraid."

"I might be able to help you with the babysitting arrangements," Alan said. "Have you considered an au pair? Belinda's met someone who's looking for a position. She's young, got plenty of energy and loves kids. She'd prefer a position where she could live in, so there'd be no problem with your hours."

It sounded like a great idea but Rachel still wasn't sure. Could she share her home with a stranger?

"I'll pay half her wages if that's what's bothering you," Alan offered. "It's only fair, they're my kids too."

Actually, it wasn't fair. Len wasn't his and he'd be the one needing the most looking after. "It's a good idea but I'll have to think about it. I can't make up my mind just like that, particularly as it's not something I've considered."

"You could always meet her," Alan suggested. "Tomorrow evening sound okay?"

What option did she have? Rachel shrugged. "Why not?"

"Perfect, and we'll have Len again tomorrow. No arguments. Belinda was in her element today. A woman stopped her on the High Street and asked if he was her grandson."

"And she didn't mind?"

"No, quite the opposite. She dotes on the little fella."

"What's her name, the au pair?"

"Sofia Henshall, and I promise you'll like her. Belinda does."

With a quick peck on the cheek, Alan was gone. Rachel stood, thinking about his suggestion. She'd discuss it with Mia and then decide. On the plus side it would solve the childcare problem, and having someone live in would give her the freedom she had enjoyed when Alan lived next door.

"Homework's done," Mia announced. "Can I go to Chloe's now? Her dad'll bring me back later."

"Okay. Taken your insulin, have you?"

"Yes, Mum. I know what I'm doing. It's not a problem."

Mia had always coped well with her diabetes, which was a blessing, but it didn't stop Rachel worrying. "Your dad's suggested we have someone live in, an au pair. What d'you think?"

"Cool. That stuck-up Amy Brandt's parents have one. That'll show her she's not so special."

Rachel rolled her eyes. So, she needn't have worried. "Okay, I'll discuss it further with your dad tomorrow."

CHAPTER NINE

Tuesday

No sooner had Rachel sat down in her office the following morning than she received a call from Jude.

"We have a problem," Jude began. "A real puzzler and it'll take some working out. Could you and Elwyn get down here as soon as possible?"

Jude was definitely not her usual easy-going self. She spoke urgently, in clipped tones.

Intrigued, Rachel said, "What? No clues?"

"I wouldn't know where to begin," Jude admitted. "It's an anomaly I've never encountered before."

An anomaly. Most mysterious — so much so that at first Rachel thought her friend was joking. But Jude sounded deadly serious. "Okay, we'll be there as soon as."

Rachel went out into the main office for a quick briefing with the team.

"Right, what have we got?" She looked at Jonny. "The good reverend. What's his story?"

"Nothing exciting, ma'am. He's been at Ancoats for twenty years. Prior to that he was at a church in Oldham. He never married, had a housekeeper who's since died, and he'll be retiring next year."

"And you're sure that's all there is? Dug deep enough, have you?"

"I reckon so. He's not a suspect, is he?"

"Until we know different, everyone's a suspect at this point. Now, Mary's friends." Rachel looked at Amy.

"In the last few years she'd spent most of her time with Dorothea Hart. They've known each other since their schooldays, and until Mary's death, they lived in the same block of flats and shared similar interests. Dorothea has one son living in Canada and has no record, neither does her dead husband or the son. Oh, and she's been released from hospital," Amy said.

Model citizens in other words. All very well, but it gave them nothing to go on. "You two, continue digging, particularly where the vicar is concerned. I want to know everything you can unearth about that man. Elwyn and I have a date with Jude. We'll meet back here at lunchtime to discuss what we've got."

"Has Jude got something for us already?" Elwyn asked as they crossed the car park.

"I'm not sure. She's discovered something but wants to discuss it in person. She was at her most enigmatic, and that worries me. Jude doesn't do drama."

"I just hope that whatever it is, it helps us find who killed Mary Dunn."

* * *

Jude was probably the finest forensic scientist Rachel's team had ever worked with, and they had complete confidence in her. Rachel wasn't aware of it yet, but what Jude was about to tell them this morning would stretch their faith in her to the limit.

As soon as they arrived, Jude ushered them into her office, told them to sit and poured them coffee. Her silence, the look on her face, told Rachel this was serious.

"Do you recall the John Lawson case?" Jude began.

The name did ring a bell. Rachel strove to retrieve it from the back of her mind. It took a few seconds, and then there it was, complete with blood and gore. "Not a case I worked on, thankfully. He was the killer known as the 'Ancoats Slasher' wasn't he?"

Jude nodded. "Well remembered since it was fifteen years ago. His last victim was found stabbed and cut to pieces on the floor of his kitchen. The house in question was in a terrace of ten off Pollard Street. The entire street has long since been cleared and now several high-rise apartment blocks have taken their place. But rest assured, at the time there was plenty forensic evidence to make the charges against Lawson stick."

"The Slasher was caught trying to flee the country as I remember," Rachel said.

"That's right. About to drive onto a ferry at Dover. He was arrested, tried, found guilty and jailed. The man was a loner and wasn't any different in prison. He made enemies, rubbed people up the wrong way and it wasn't long before he got himself beaten up. In the first six months of his sentence, Lawson suffered a number of injuries at the hands of fellow inmates. The crunch came one night when one of them set a fire in Lawson's cell. He was in it. Following his death there was a huge outcry — he'd barely started his sentence and his victims felt cheated."

Details about the case came slowly trickling back. Although Rachel hadn't worked it herself, she had been aware of the chatter and the huge amount of paperwork it generated — she'd had to file some of it. Then there was the publicity. It seemed that not a day went by when it wasn't headline news.

"The last victim, Holroyd. Wasn't there a suspicion that he was connected to the Slasher in some way?" Elwyn said.

"Yes, but nothing was proved," Jude said. "Without further evidence it couldn't be taken any further. Anyway, the man was dead. Despite being questioned about him at the trial, Lawson refused to say anything to implicate Holroyd."

"As I remember it, the Slasher couldn't drive so he needed an accomplice to get him around. There was also the matter of dumping the bodies. At least three of them were not killed where they were found. Holroyd was young and strong enough to have helped him," Elwyn said. "It seemed a reasonable assumption."

Rachel was getting confused. This was all very interesting but what was the point? "How is this story about a killer from the past connected with the murder of Mary?"

"A couple of hours ago, I got the result of the DNA tests I did." Jude paused, an odd look on her face. "To be honest, I'm still reeling from what it told me. I've never had anything like this happen before and it's come as quite a shock."

She paused, looking from Rachel to Elwyn. "The DNA I extracted from the hairs found on Mary's clothing is an exact match for that of John Lawson, a killer who, fifteen years ago, stalked these streets. The man who was known as the 'Ancoats Slasher'."

CHAPTER TEN

"But how can that be?" Rachel asked, totally mystified. "Lawson is dead, you said so yourself."

Jude shrugged. Truth was, she had no idea. "I will repeat the test but I doubt the result will be any different."

"It doesn't make sense. You're telling me we're chasing a dead man."

Elwyn took the report from Jude. "It's all here, Rachel, and science doesn't lie."

"No, but people do." What Jude had told them meant there was something seriously amiss in the way that case had been handled. "We need to take another look at that old case. Given that Mary wasn't stabbed by a ghost, we've got a lot of work ahead of us. For starters, we need to find out a great deal more about Lawson. That's where the mistake lies, I'll stake my career on it."

"I don't recall the case," Jude said. "Fifteen years is a long time and forensic science has improved. Still, I don't see how it was possible to catch and jail the wrong man, even back then."

"Nonetheless, if your latest test is to be believed that's exactly what happened," Rachel said.

"I have no explanation, Rachel."

"I don't understand it either. I mean there were plenty of people at Lawson's trial, local people who would have recognised him. Surely someone would have spoken up if they saw the wrong man in the dock?" Rachel took a deep breath. She could have done without this. "What, I wonder, does this have to do with Mary Dunn? Is it possible that she's connected to the Slasher case in some way?"

"That's for you to check out," Jude said. "You could start by looking at her relatives and friends. See if any of them was a victim of the Slasher, or if Mary had any connection to Lawson."

Rachel drained her coffee and got to her feet. "Run the test again, simply for completeness, but for now we'll work on the basis that the result is correct and look into what really happened to John Lawson. If your DNA result is above board and proves that he didn't die like everyone thought he did, I want to know why we were led to believe that he had. If we agree with the original conclusion that he did, then we need to know who is playing games with us."

"If you get anything, please let me know," Jude said. "This one could well keep me awake nights. Not to mention that we possibly have a killer active on our patch. One who's been 'resting' these last fifteen years."

Jude's information left Rachel feeling like she had a deep pit to climb out of. "This is going to mean a hellava lot of work," she said to Elwyn as they drove away from the morgue.

"And makes finding Mary's killer no easier."

"We'll have a quick word with Dorothea Hart on our way back to the station. You never know, she may be able to throw some light on it all," Rachel said.

* * *

Several of the residents were gathered in Dorothea's flat. News of what had happened to Mary had got round and they were all curious.

"They're a lovely bunch," Dorothea told Rachel. "They're not being ghoulish, they all loved Mary." She cast her eyes downwards. "I can't imagine what life here will be like without her. She was the glue that held everything together. Some people are like that, don't you find?"

"Are you up to answering a few questions, Mrs Hart?" Elwyn asked. "Then we'll leave you in peace."

"Ask me anything you like. I want to help — and call me Dotty, everyone does."

"Was Mary afraid of anyone?" Rachel asked.

"Not that I'm aware of. If she was, she never said anything to me, and I'm sure she would have done."

"Had she said anything about seeing anyone new, anyone from her past?"

Dotty shook her head but after thinking for a moment, said, "Ah, wait. Funnily enough, she did start looking through her old photos — her albums and that. I asked her if there was anything in particular she was looking for, and could I help, but she laughed it off. She said it was probably her imagination. Anyway, I wouldn't know the person."

"This person, was it someone she might have known years ago?"

"Possibly," Dotty said. "Her memory was bad. Looking through those photos brought things back. But one night she got quite upset. She talked about her husband and daughter, and a man she'd not seen in years."

"Why was she upset? Did she think Kimberley was in some sort of danger?"

"No, it wasn't that. It was about something that had happened in the past, I think."

Rachel felt Elwyn's hand on her shoulder. "That's enough for now," he said softly.

Fair enough. The elderly woman had had a shock and was no doubt tired. "We'll leave you in peace. If you remember anything, Dotty, anything at all, or if you just want to chat about Mary, ring this number," Rachel said, handing her a card. "We will do our level best to catch whoever did this to your friend."

"Such wickedness, and in a church too. I can't get over it. Mary never harmed a fly."

"D'you know Kimberley and her son?"

"Yes, although we've not seen much of Kim since she took up with that new man of hers. As for the boy, I suppose he'll come good one day."

"This new man of Kimberley's, d'you mean Jack Fairhurst?"

"That's him. Strange man, too quiet for my liking. Not Kim's usual sort at all." Dotty took a framed photo off the sideboard. "This is Mary with Kim and Jack. It was only taken a month ago at a christening we went to."

Rachel took a good look. "D'you mind if I borrow this? I promise you'll get it back."

"Certainly, if it helps," Dotty said.

"Thank you, Dotty. You've been a great help."

Rachel and Elwyn walked back along the corridor.

"This boyfriend, Fairhurst, we should do a full background check," Rachel told Elwyn. "See if there's anything lurking in his past." She handed him the photo. "He looks about fifty, and the hair colour's a match too. Or am I asking too much?"

"If he killed Mary, that makes him the Slasher. But if the real slasher was not the one imprisoned fifteen years ago, the one with his photo in all the papers, how would Mary know him?" Elwyn said.

"Sorry, I should have thought it through. But we'll take a look at him anyway."

CHAPTER ELEVEN

Back at the station Rachel went to her office, logged onto the database, and quickly apprised herself of the basics of the 'Slasher' case. It didn't make comfortable reading. The Slasher — or John Lawson — was a cold-blooded killer who showed no remorse. But at least in the end he had the good grace to admit his guilt — but not why he did it. He was believed to have chosen his victims at random. Was that what Mary was? Had she presented the killer with an opportunity he couldn't pass up? But why now? It was fifteen years since Lawson last struck, so what had motivated him now?

Ten minutes later, Rachel gathered the team together in the incident room. They knew she had received an urgent call from Jude and waited with interest to hear what she'd had to say.

"We've had the initial DNA results back from the lab," Rachel began. "The good news is that we now have a name for Mary Dunn's killer."

A small cheer went up and Jonny Farrell's face broke into a grin. "Not so bad after all, this job. When the science works, it really works."

Rachel raised her hand. "Don't get carried away. You haven't heard the bad news yet."

As she spoke, Superintendent Mark Kenton slunk quietly into the room and, as was his habit, stood at the back.

"The killer is one John Lawson." Rachel paused, giving them a moment to think. It had been a huge case in its time. It was possible that one of them had heard or read about it, but their faces were blank.

"About fifteen years ago, a killer known as the 'Ancoats Slasher' stalked the streets of Ancoats and its surrounds. He was thirty-five years old, single and unemployed. People who knew him thought him a pleasant man who lived a fairly simple life and minded his own business. Little did they know. Lawson was in fact a sadistic killer who managed to evade capture for two long years. Eventually, after stabbing four victims, he was caught, tried, found guilty and subsequently murdered in prison."

"A fascinating story, but where does this John Lawson fit into our case, ma'am?" Amy asked.

Rachel glanced round at their expectant faces, including that of Kenton. They weren't going to believe this. Thank goodness she had science on her side.

"John Lawson's DNA was found on Mary Dunn's body," she said.

No one spoke as they all processed this. Finally, Amy broke the silence.

"How can that be, ma'am? You just told us he died in prison," she said.

"Someone died in prison, Amy, someone that may or may not have been Lawson. Jude assures me that although she'll repeat the test, there's no mistake with the DNA. It tells us that Lawson is our killer. Unless someone is playing some elaborate game, that means the man arrested, tried and imprisoned all those years ago has to have been someone else. Or he was substituted for someone else along the way. Lawson is still alive and we have to find him. The Slasher case is fifteen years old and Lawson will have aged, perhaps deliberately changed his appearance, meaning we have no idea what he looks like today. Given what happened, we might not even know what he looked like back then."

"I recall the case," Kenton suddenly piped up from the back. "There is a mountain of paperwork associated with it, boxes of evidence stored away. But for a first-hand account, the man to speak to is Superintendent Hedley Sharpe. He too is in Serious Crime and works out of the station in Old Trafford. He was a DS back then, but the SIO has since died. I reckon he's the only one left who can help you."

"Thanks, sir," Rachel said. "I'll have that word. All the paperwork will have to be looked at. Someone lied when it came to identifying Lawson. I want to speak to that person first and find out why."

"You do realise that person may be dead, don't you? I'll draft in some help. You're going to need it," Kenton said.

Rachel thanked him again, he wasn't wrong there. She turned back to the team. "First, we'll seek out anyone who gave a statement, was associated with one of the victims or who was interviewed at the time, to see if any of them had a connection to Mary." She looked at Amy. "Contact Superintendent Sharpe and arrange for me to see him." Next, she addressed one of the uniformed members of the team. "Arrange to have everything on that case taken out of storage and brought up to the office."

Finally, she turned to Elwyn. "We'll find out what we can about Fairhurst, Kimberley Dunn's new boyfriend. He's the right age and it's possible that Mary recognised him. She had lived in Ancoats all her life and she may have been privy to all kinds of gossip about that case, and even Lawson himself."

Her team looked at each other, stunned, as they realised how much work this was going to mean. Rachel clapped her hands. "Okay, get to it."

She went to her office and sat down at her computer to take another look at the online case file. Kenton wasn't wrong, there was reams of the stuff. She leaned back in her chair and closed her eyes. She needed to concentrate on what was important. The crux of the case was Lawson's motive for targeting Mary now. Did he know her? Had something arisen from the past that had prompted him to kill her? If this was the case, at least the team would have something to work with. She was filled with dread at the thought that Lawson had picked up where he'd left off and chosen her at random.

If that was the case, the big question was why now? Why start again and in the same location as before? Was it possible that Lawson had recently returned to the area for some reason? If he had, he was taking a risk. It had been a long time but someone might recognise him. Is that what happened with Mary? On the other hand, the world thought him dead. Did he believe he could kill safe in the knowledge that no one would point the finger? Recent advances in forensics and DNA technology could well have passed him by.

Too many questions and not enough answers. And to crown it all was Rachel's growing belief that she was no longer up to the job. A problem she needed to sort, and quick. If she decided the job was too much for her and she'd reached the end of the road, it would mean a drastic change to all their lives. She'd spent last night studying the property market and was confident the cottage would realise enough for her and the kids to make a fresh start somewhere new, unconnected in any way with the police force. But was that the right thing to do? It was tantamount to running away, and not her style at all.

Elwyn burst into her office, a broad grin on his face. "Fairhurst doesn't have a record but he is known. He beat up a man in the local pub one night, and when the man's mother tried to intervene, he clobbered her too. Problem is the injured parties didn't press charges, so he was never convicted."

"Still, that means he's not averse to using violence," Rachel said. "We need another word with Kimberley about her mother. We'll speak to him too. Where do we find him?"

"As Kimberley said, Fairhurst is unemployed. We'll speak to her first and go from there."

Rachel grabbed her jacket and pocketed her mobile. "What's your instinct telling you, Elwyn?"

"Not a lot. We can't even be sure if Lawson had a motive for killing Mary. We just don't know enough. If there is one, finding it will go a long way in finding Lawson."

Rachel grimaced. "I've just been picturing the horror of having another serial killer on the patch."

Elwyn nodded. "All the Slasher's victims were women except for Holroyd. We've nothing on why he killed him but at the time it added credibility to the notion of Holroyd as his accomplice. Lawson, everyone believed, was making his getaway and tidying up, making sure he left no loose ends. As for the details, Lawson always tied his victims' hands with white ribbon and left them holding a white rose."

"The gaffer tape?"

"That too."

"Were all those details general knowledge at the time?" Rachel asked.

"Yes, it was all written up in the press," Elwyn said.

"Why Mary, Elwyn? Could she have known him?"

"We can't make assumptions, Rachel. There may be a reason why Mary was targeted, or maybe there isn't. But if there is, I reckon it has to be rooted in the past, and that's where we should be looking."

"Lawson killed four women followed by Holroyd. We don't want another spate of killings like that. A serial killer is not on my wish list at the moment."

"You asked about my instincts, well, they're telling me it's more complex than that."

He could be right. Rachel was about to add something when Elwyn's mobile rang.

Smiling, he half turned away from Rachel. "Tina, you can relax, I managed to get the tickets after all. I'll pick you up at seven."

Rachel wandered off towards the car, leaving Elwyn to chat alone. Who was Tina, and why hadn't he mentioned her?

He caught up with her, still smiling. "New friend?" Rachel asked.

He looked embarrassed. "Sort of, but it's early days. A bit like your new relationship. You know me, Rachel. I'm not much good with women. Look what happened with Marie."

He was talking about his ex-wife. "What're the tickets for?"

"The theatre tonight."

"Sounds pretty good to me."

CHAPTER TWELVE

Rachel and Elwyn set off to find Kimberley and Fairhurst. "We don't have a lot to go on," Elwyn said. "Fairhurst is the right age, his hair is the right colour and he likes to beat people up. Not good, I'll give you that, but does it make him the man we're after?"

"Lawson must have chosen Mary for a reason," Rachel said, "and it's interesting that Fairhurst is Kimberley's new boyfriend. Maybe he got together with her because Mary recognised him from the past. Granted it's very tenuous, but we have to start somewhere. Shame he wasn't arrested for that assault, we'd have his DNA then, and could check it against what we've got. But we'll ask him if he'd mind giving us a sample."

"First her son, Ronan, and now we go after the man in her life. Poor old Kimberley." Elwyn sighed. "I reckon this is a lot more complex than that. Have you considered the unfinished business theory?"

"We don't know that Lawson had any unfinished business. We do know, however, that he chose his victims at random," Rachel said.

"That's what they thought at the time but given that we're taking another look, I reckon we should keep an open mind. According to what I've read in the file, Lawson said very little about his victims during the interviews. He was asked why he chose them but never gave a straight answer."

Elwyn was right, of course. Who knew what went on in the mind of a killer? Lawson's reasons for murdering his victims would be complex, could be rooted in any aspect of his life.

* * *

The pair were lucky, they found Jack Fairhurst sitting on Kimberley's sofa. He was nervous and the moment they walked into the room, he jumped up and started to pace like a trapped animal.

"I know what this is. Police harassment. I get done once and you're at my door for every little thing that cracks off."

"That's not true, Mr Fairhurst," Rachel said. "We simply want to ask you a couple of questions."

"Sit down, Jack," Kimberley said. "This is about my mother, not you."

"Where were you living before you moved in with Kimberley?" Elwyn asked.

"My brother's place in Longsight. That was until he got a job on the rigs up in the north of Scotland."

"Work?"

Fairhurst gave a humourless laugh. "Not at the moment, pal. Though I have got an interview next week at the soap place where Kim works. Pay's rubbish but at least it's money coming in. In the meantime, I've been doing the odd job for that vicar at the church. Mary put in a good word for me."

"How do you find Neville?" Rachel asked.

"Weird. He wants jobs doing but won't let me go into certain areas of the church — that back room of his being one."

"Has he said why?" Rachel asked.

Fairhurst grunted. "He's not the type for explanations."

"Mr Fairhurst, can you recall where you were living and working fifteen years ago?" Elwyn asked him.

He laughed. "I can barely remember where I was last week. Why? Is it important?"

"Could be."

"I was a lot younger, I know that. Fifteen years is a lifetime." He scratched his head. "Fifteen years . . . that was about the time me and my bro did the grape harvest in the Loire Valley in France. We started off working on the Costas and moved north when the harvest was due in. In fact, for two years we were hardly in this country at all."

"Can you prove that?" Rachel asked.

He shook his head. "I doubt it. I might have the odd photo or two lurking in one of my old cameras, but you'll have to give me time to look for them. I've no receipts or anything. I wouldn't have kept them that long, and anyway, we were paid in cash — euros — and most weeks we spent the lot."

"Where did you live?" Elwyn asked.

"We were given accommodation during the grape-picking. We both worked the bars on the Costas and again we were given a room. We weren't fussy. All we needed was a place to put our heads down."

"I want you to have a good look and see if you can find anything that proves your story."

Fairhurst looked at Rachel. "Look, love, it's no story, it's the truth. I was never one for settling down, not until recently." He took hold of Kimberley's hand. "But things are different now. I'm making a new start."

"Would you mind giving us a sample of your DNA, Mr Fairhurst?" Elwyn asked. "It's a swab from the inside of your cheek and only takes a second. We may need it for elimination purposes, given you must have visited Mary's flat a few times."

Fairhurst's face clouded over. "Why should I? I've done nowt. What exactly are you eliminating me from? What am I supposed to have done?"

"You're not supposed to have done anything, Mr Fairhurst. We just want to rule people in or out," Rachel said.

"This is about Mary's murder, isn't it? You lot think I did for the old woman." He looked at Kimberley. "This is bullshit, you know that. Tell them where we were Sunday night, love."

"We went to the cinema in Manchester and then on to a club. We didn't get back here till about two in the morning. Jack was with me all the time, there was no way he could have killed my mother."

Fairhurst was still glaring at the pair. "All right? Go on then, take your bloody sample. Let's sort this once and for all."

CHAPTER THIRTEEN

Outside Kimberley's house, Rachel and Elwyn sat in the car for a moment or two. "What d'you think?" Elwyn asked.

"He talks the talk, I know that, but we have the sample. Once Jude has done her stuff, we'll know the truth. What he told us about the church is interesting though."

Rachel turned on the ignition and they moved off. As they turned onto the ring road, her private mobile rang in her bag.

"If he's telling the truth," Elwyn said. "Where to now?"

"Let's see what's happening at the graveyard. Jude and her team have been at it most of the day, she may have something."

The ringing stopped but then started up again. "Get that for me, will you? Unless it's one of the girls, tell whoever it is I'll ring them back."

Elwyn fished the phone from her bag and listened, a grin spreading across his face. "That was one David Pearson. Says he is a friend."

Rachel gave him a quick glance. "That's right. He's the guy I met in North Wales. His brother is a member of the boating club near your parents' bungalow."

"Spend a lot of time together, did you?"

"Enough to realise that we had stuff in common. He's a friend, easy to talk to and like me, he has a few problems. Look, Elwyn, there's nothing in it. The minute there is, you'll be the first to know."

Elwyn remained silent during the half a mile or so to the church. As Rachel parked up, they saw the forensic team hard at work. "I'll have a word with Jude, then we'll drop Fairhurst's sample off at the lab."

"A number of footprints in the mud," began Jude at once. "They match the mud found inside the church and could belong to our killer. We've taken casts, so we might be able to work out what footwear he had on."

"Anything around Mary's husband's grave?" Rachel asked.

"Nothing, only the rose petals and the empty vase. It's gone in for fingerprint analysis."

"Anything else strike you as significant?" Rachel asked.

"There was something, actually." Jude smiled. "It might mean nothing, but there again . . . who knows?" She led the way along the row of graves and stopped at a fairly recent one. "The vicar tells me the permanent headstone will be laid sometime in the near future. But you can see her name on the wooden plaque."

Rachel bent down for a look. "Tara Shepherd. Who is she?"

"It says here she died three months ago. She was sixty-six, a widow of this parish," Jude said. "Married to Douglas."

Rachel looked down at the plot. The roses in the vase appeared to be the same as the one Mary had in her hands. If that was so, the killer had taken the roses from Albert Dunn's grave and put all but one of them on this one. Why? Rachel looked at Elwyn. "When we get back to the station, we should find out all we can about Tara Shepherd. It might be important, it might not, but we can't afford to ignore any detail. Also, we'll see if the vicar can tell us anything about this woman's funeral — who attended, who sent flowers, that sort of thing."

"Want a word with him now?" he asked.

Rachel nodded. Why not? She found the man strangely creepy but couldn't avoid him. He could be an important piece of the puzzle.

* * *

"It was a quiet affair as I recall, only a handful of mourners. Her son, a few friends, and some of the congregation from here."

"Would that have included Mary?" Rachel asked.

"Yes, she and Dotty were both here. Mary knew Tara from years ago, although she did tell me that the woman had become something of a recluse in recent times."

"Why was that, d'you know?"

Henry Neville shrugged. "I presume that after her husband died, she didn't feel confident going out on her own and being with people. They were very much a couple, did everything together, so I was told."

"Odd that he's not buried here," Elwyn noted.

"His wishes were to be cremated and his ashes scattered in Morecambe, his favourite seaside town. Tara was against cremation. Her parents are in this graveyard, over there, I believe." He pointed.

"Can you shed any light on why the white roses on Albert Dunn's grave were transferred to Tara Shepherd's?"

Henry Neville looked at Rachel blankly. "I didn't realise they had. I'm sorry, I can offer no explanation."

From the look on his face, they weren't going to get anything more out of him. "Okay, thanks for your help," Rachel said.

The vicar pointed towards the forensic technicians still working in the graveyard. "When will they be gone?"

"I don't know. When they've finished, I suppose," Rachel said. "But don't worry. They will leave the place exactly as they found it."

"Have they discovered anything useful?"

She smiled. "I'm not sure. I'll have to wait for the report." Even if Jude had found something, there was no way Rachel was going to share it with the vicar. The uneasy feeling she had about him was even stronger today.

"Vicar or not, that's one strange man," she whispered to Elwyn as they walked off. "It's definitely his eyes — they're dark, evil."

"You're letting your imagination run away with you."

But Rachel knew she wasn't. The feeling was real. She checked the time. It was late in the afternoon. "I've got to get home," she said. "I'm considering getting an au pair — Alan's idea, not mine. I'm meeting the young woman tonight and I want the place to look half decent. She might be the answer to my problem and I don't want my messy house putting her off."

"Sounds like a good idea. I'll drop you at the station and you can get off. I'll make a start on finding out about Tara Shepherd and bring you up to speed in the morning."

CHAPTER FOURTEEN

Back in the incident room, Elwyn tasked the team with finding out everything they could about Tara Shepherd. Neither Jonny nor Amy were particularly impressed when he told them why.

"Grasping at straws," Jonny commented. "So, the guy steals a single rose from a bunch and dumps the remaining blooms as he walks into the church. What was he supposed to do with them?"

"Why not just chuck them away?" Elwyn said. "But he didn't. He took the trouble to put them in a vase on another grave. Rachel doesn't want anything overlooked, so we check. All right?"

"I have a date tonight," Amy moaned. "This job just gets worse. Where's her ladyship anyway? I don't see her mucking in."

"You'd do well to keep comments like that to yourself," Elwyn said. "Rachel or Kenton hear you and you won't be popular round here."

Jonny's head was down, eyes glued to his screen. "Well, that didn't take long," he said shortly. "I've got a hit. Tara Shepherd née Lawson, would you believe. According to her birth record and that of John Lawson, the two were siblings, same parents. She was older than him."

So, Elwyn realised, he'd put the flowers on his sister's grave. He wondered if Lawson had attended the funeral. "Keep digging, there may be more." If this was down to Lawson then someone from the neighbourhood must have told him about Tara's death. Possibly he'd stayed in touch with friends or family, if there was any. "Did Tara have any other family?" he asked.

"Tara had a son, Daniel Shepherd. He lives in Bright House, that new apartment block. It's the one where Arlo Bain, our young dealer, lives."

A connection? It was a coincidence and one they'd have to explore. "Those apartments are pricy," Elwyn said. "Find out how this son earns his money."

"Hang on," Jonny said. "There's another sister — Lauren."

"Surname?" Elwyn asked.

"Gilbert. Married to Jacob."

That was bad news. Elwyn was only too aware of who Jacob Gilbert was, and of their suspicions about him. "John Lawson, Tara Shepherd and Lauren Gilbert. That it?"

"Looks like it. Want me to look into the Gilberts' past?"

"No need. We already know that following the demise of Grace Blackmore and her cohorts, Jacob is the new gangster on the block. I'll wager there's a file on him as long as your arm but little to take to the CPS. If the Gilberts are involved in any way, we'll have to tread careful."

The vicar had told them that both Mary and Dotty had been at Tara's funeral. Elwyn wondered how much of the event Dotty might remember. Had Mary recognised Lauren? Was that what had put her in danger? He and Rachel would call at Dotty's flat in the morning and speak to her. He'd give Rachel a ring later and tell her what they'd got.

"Good work, folks," he flexed his fingers and began updating the case notes. He nodded at Jonny. "Find out if there's anything else we should know about both Tara and Lauren. We'll give it another half hour and then call it a day." Amy wasn't the only one with a date tonight. He was off to the theatre with Tina, and he didn't want to be late.

* * *

Megan was out when Rachel came home. She'd left a hastily scrawled note on the kitchen table to say that she wouldn't be back tonight. Mia was round at Chloe's — where else — and Len was sleeping peacefully in his pram for once. Belinda certainly had a magic touch, something Rachel could do with borrowing.

In an effort to impress the girl, she hastily tidied up and ran the vacuum cleaner over the sitting-room floor. There wasn't time to do much else. Finally, she put the coffee on and waited. Belinda had gone to pick up Sofia from the railway station and they'd be back any time.

Rachel appreciated Belinda's help but she still felt incredibly guilty at having to hire someone to take care of her kids. Though if she wanted to continue working, what choice did she have?

She heard Belinda's car draw up and went to the front door. The girl who alighted from the passenger door was tall and slender with long blonde hair. She didn't look a lot older than Megan.

"This is Sofia," Belinda said with a smile. "Are the children here?"

"Len is, Mia's gone to her friend Chloe's house. She practically lives there," she said with a glance at Sofia. "And the eldest is hitting the high spots of Manchester again."

"You have a baby?" Sofia asked, ignoring Rachel's potted family history. "May I meet him?"

Rachel smiled and beckoned to her. "Len is the one who'll take up most of your time. He's at that age where he's crawling about. When he starts walking, he'll be a nightmare. It'll be eyes in the back of your head time."

None of this appeared to bother Sofia. She went over to his pram and peered in. "He is a beautiful boy. You should be proud of him."

Rachel nodded. "Beautiful he might be, but he is a handful. He doesn't usually sleep much during the day, so he'll run you ragged."

Sofia smiled. "Doesn't matter. I love children. Back home I have younger brothers and sisters. I'm used to how they are."

Rachel nodded. "You have a good grasp of English. Have you been here long?"

Sofia handed Rachel a portfolio. "Take a look through. All my experience and qualifications are in there, plus a couple of references."

"Sofia comes from an excellent background," Belinda said.

Rachel hoped so. If she took this girl on, she was entrusting her with the safekeeping of her kids. "I work long hours. Sometimes I'm not back until late evening. You'd be required to feed them, bathe Len and put him to bed. Can you manage that?"

"Yes, of course," she said. "I will also keep an eye on the younger teen. Ensure she abides by your rules."

Rachel laughed. "If you can do that you'll be worth your weight in gold. Mia has diabetes, type one, and is on daily insulin. She's very good at dealing with the injections and can be left to manage. A gentle reminder is needed sometimes though." She flicked through the portfolio. "Look, let me go through this tonight. I won't keep you waiting now. I'll let Belinda know one way or other in the morning. If I do take you on, when can you start?"

"Straightaway," Sofia said.

Just what Rachel wanted to hear.

CHAPTER FIFTEEN

Wednesday

Sofia's CV was excellent. The girl had the right experience and her qualifications, gained at a college in Northumberland, were more than suitable. So much so that Rachel felt guilty at not being able to offer her a higher rate of pay. Given her situation, it was a no-brainer really. She needed someone, didn't have the time to meet and interview dozens of others, and Sofia came with Belinda's blessing. There were references in the portfolio and Rachel would give them a ring over the next couple of days. The big decision now — a start date. Sofia had said straightaway, so why not? Before she left for work, Rachel rang Belinda. "Let her know that she can bring her stuff round and start making herself at home."

"Good decision, Rachel. I'll be with you in about ten minutes. Me and Len will pick up Sofia later and I'll hang around today and show her the ropes. Len is lovely but he does have his little foibles."

"Thanks, Belinda. I'll do my best not to be late. There's a bedroom at the back of the house, it's newly decorated, has plenty of cupboard space and looks out over the garden. Tell Sofia she can have it."

Domestic stuff sorted, she grabbed her jacket and bag and was ready to leave just as Belinda pulled into the drive. A quick wave and she left her to it.

As Rachel left Poynton village, she received a call from Elwyn. She put the phone on speaker and listened to what he had to say.

"Tara Shepherd was Lawson's sister. It's only a theory, but what if he returned to Ancoats for her funeral and was recognised by Mary? I thought we'd have another word with her friends, ask if any of them went to Tara's funeral and if they recall any strangers attending. You should also know that there is another sister, none other than Lauren Gilbert, wife of the infamous Jacob."

A man who'd risen to prominence in Manchester's gangland during the months she'd been in North Wales. "After we've been to the flats we'll speak to the vicar again," Rachel decided. "After all, Tara Shepherd is buried in his graveyard. He may know more about her family."

"Good. Sounds feasible," Elwyn said.

"Tell the troops to keep digging for info and I'll meet you at the station as soon as I can get there."

Traffic would be bad at this time in the morning. It'd be nose to tail down the A6 into the city. Having someone permanent to take care of the kids, and particularly Len, was one thing, but the long drive to and from work each day had become more of a problem than it had ever been. Rachel needed to move, to leave her past — particularly that house with its assorted memories — behind. Their new home, wherever that was, would have to be a lot closer to the station. Megan wouldn't complain, she'd love being nearer the city, but Mia would miss her friends, Chloe most of all. That could turn out to be the real problem — she had been close to Chloe since her nursery days.

* * *

From the station, the pair took Elwyn's car and went to Mary's flat. There, they were met by two police cars and a cordon around the main entrance.

Flashing her warrant card, Rachel approached the uniformed officer guarding the door.

"A break-in, ma'am. Early doors we reckon. One of the tenants heard a noise, went to investigate and got a whack across the head for his trouble."

The pair followed the officer inside and up the stairs. Mary Dunn's flat had been turned upside down. Every drawer and cupboard had been opened and its contents strewn across the floor.

"Forensics been?" Rachel asked, pulling on a pair of nitrile gloves.

"Due any time, ma'am."

"Who got hurt?" Elwyn asked.

"One of the old boys, a Reg Hitchin."

Rachel swallowed. She'd met Reg, he was frail and no match for whoever had done this. Having found the front door unlocked that time, she should have left an officer here to keep watch. It was an omission she now regretted and could only hope it didn't come back to haunt her. "Any idea how he is?"

"He's been carted off in an ambulance, ma'am."

"Okay. We'll take it from here."

Rachel paced around the small apartment, picked up a photo with the glass broken and placed it on the sideboard. "What were they looking for, Elwyn? What could Mary possibly have had to cause an old man to get beaten up and her property ransacked like this?"

"We had a look around, and didn't find anything of value," Elwyn said.

"Not to us, maybe, but whoever did this was looking for something. And we have to find out what it was."

"Perhaps it was the photographs he was after, what d'you think?" Elwyn said.

"Some of them were years old. You might be right. Whoever did this could be afraid that he featured in one and might be recognised." She looked at him. "You're thinking Lawson, or whoever is making us think he's still alive, aren't you? You think he did this."

"Lawson, or someone close to him, is tied into this case somehow. And who else would have an interest in Mary's possessions? Her family perhaps, but they wouldn't have turned the place upside down. And Mary had nothing to attract the attention of a burglar."

Rachel nodded. Probably, though she would keep an open mind. "Let's have a chat with the others, see what they can tell us."

* * *

Dotty had gathered everyone together in the communal sitting room and was busy serving tea.

"We've had a terrible shock," she said to Rachel. "Thankfully, Reg is going to be all right. I've rung the hospital and he's out of danger."

That was a relief. "Did anyone see or hear anything?" Rachel asked the semi-circle of residents. There was a unanimous shaking of heads. "Dotty, you must know Mary's flat pretty well. When our forensics people have finished, I'd like you to take a look and tell us if there's anything missing."

Dotty nodded. "Yes, of course. Anything we can do to help."

Rachel looked at the assembled group. "Are any of you familiar with the name John Lawson?"

There was a chorus of mutters. "The Slasher," Dotty said with a shudder. "Mary knew him, knew his sisters Tara and Lauren too. But this can't have anything to do with him, he died in that prison — murdered so I read."

Rachel said yes, she didn't want any speculation at this point. "Did Mary ever talk about him?"

Dotty gave her a thoughtful look. "I don't know if it was him she meant, but she did say something. I thought it was odd at the time. We'd been cleaning the church. The reverend had someone with him, and they were arguing in the back. Mary got a bit nervous, said she recognised the voice. I asked who it was, and she said it was best I didn't

68

know." She smiled painfully at the pair. "Always thoughtful like that was Mary. Anyway, I kept on and finally she said he was a bad 'un from a while back and not to get involved. I didn't understand, so I dropped it. But it bothered me. Mary had made out that the man was older, like us, but I was sure whoever was speaking was young. I didn't say anything, I thought it best not to. Three days later we went to Tara's funeral. Mary got very upset and pointed out a man to me. She said he gave her the creeps. Then she made me promise not to let on to anyone that we'd seen him."

"Did she say who he was? What he'd done?"

"No, only that he was evil and not to go near. She could be like that could Mary."

CHAPTER SIXTEEN

Within the hour, Jude and her team were at Mary's flat. Rachel asked her if she'd got anything unusual when she first dusted for prints.

"No. If there was someone here the night Mary was killed, they left no trace, other than the unlocked door." Jude shook her head. "Which could simply have been a mistake on Mary's part."

"Well, what's happened now is no mistake," Rachel said. "Someone has given the place a right going over."

"If they've left any trace at all this time, we'll find it," Jude said.

The trouble was, Rachel had no idea what they'd been looking for. What was it? What had Mary seen, or had in her possession, that had made her a target for murder? And now this. "What d'you reckon, Elwyn? Some stranger chancing his luck, or does it have something to do with what happened to Mary?"

"Could be either. This block is well managed and kept nice but there are any number of scallies in the area. They get word of an empty flat and that's enough to make it a target," Elwyn said.

Rachel wasn't so sure. "Let's leave Jude to it, see what she comes up with, while have that word with the vicar."

"Your au pair turn up?" Elwyn asked.

"Her name is Sofia Henshall. Belinda should have picked her up by now. She's kindly agreed to spend the day showing her the ropes. I met the girl last night. She's okay — well qualified, young, and she seems to have plenty of energy. If she settles, it should work out just fine."

He raised his eyebrows. "And you're okay with the arrangement?"

"What choice do I have? I either keep working or I don't, and you know what the job's like. What with my childcare problems, all the driving to and from home, the entire thing's a bloody nightmare. At least now I know the kids are okay. But I'm not stupid. Her qualifications may be fine on paper but not in practice. I'll just have to see."

They pulled up outside the church, where part of the graveyard was still taped off. "What d'you reckon Neville is playing at, if anything?" Elwyn asked.

"The man is telling us the bare minimum. I reckon he has something to hide," Rachel said.

"Or he could be scared. He knows who Tara Shepherd is related to, and the Gilberts do not have a good reputation to put it mildly. You cross them at your peril."

Rachel gave a little shudder. She'd had a bellyful of Manchester's gangland of late. "Perhaps, but his caginess isn't helping the case."

The pair went inside to find the Reverend Henry Neville setting out hymn books on the pews.

"Choir practice," he said. "I presume I'm allowed to continue as normal."

Rachel nodded. "We've got a few more questions if you don't mind."

"Of course. Anything I can do to help."

"Tara Shepherd. She's buried in your graveyard. Do you know any other members of her family?"

"I knew her husband, even though he wasn't a regular here. I know she has a son. Had him late, when she was in her forties. He lives in those expensive apartments — Bright House. He doesn't come to church."

"Have you ever met him?" Rachel asked.

"Only the once, at Tara's funeral."

"What about the other sister, Lauren Gilbert?"

Neville backed off, shaking his head. "Not in here, please. That family is evil. You do know who they are — Lauren and her husband."

"Yes, which is why I'd like to know if *you* know them."

"They've never been here," he said. "Never once have they set foot inside my church."

"Not even when you buried Lauren's sister?"

"Sorry, yes, I was forgetting. She came, he didn't. Look, it was just the once, and I doubt either of them will be back. Neither of them are churchgoers, so why would they?"

"Did Lauren ever live round here?" Rachel asked.

"Yes, years ago. All the Lawson children were born two streets away."

"In that case you must have known John, too. At the very least seen him around."

"No, not really. He's been dead fifteen years, and anyway, he never attended church. I've only been here twenty years myself. The only member of that family who did attend was Tara. She was a good woman. I have come to suspect that she knew her two siblings were dangerous people, which is why she kept away from them."

"Have you any idea why someone would ransack Mary's home?" Elwyn asked.

He shook his head but, strangely, he didn't look surprised. "She had no valuables, that I do know."

"Do you have any objection to our people conducting a thorough search of the church?"

This time Henry Neville did react. He looked stunned. "Why . . . why would you want to do that?"

"Well, whoever broke into Mary's flat went through everything she possessed. They were looking for something

72

and it strikes me that whatever it was, Mary could have hidden it here."

He shook his head. "More upheaval for my congregation. Are you sure it's absolutely necessary? The place is cleaned regularly I'm sure if Mary had hidden something it would have been found by now."

"Is that a 'no'? We can always get a warrant," Rachel said.

"Okay, if you must search, then go ahead. When will you start?"

"First thing in the morning," Rachel said.

Neville heaved a sigh. Her request obviously made him anxious, and Rachel wondered why. They weren't accusing him of anything, the disruption would be minimal. All her instincts told her he was keeping something back. Well, she meant to get to the bottom of it. They would take this church apart stone by stone if necessary.

"Meanwhile, you find any more odd characters dealing drugs in your churchyard, be sure to give us a ring," she told him. "There are a couple of people in the neighbourhood I'm keen to get a word with. We'll see you in the morning."

Rachel turned on her heel and left.

* * *

"I thought Kenton told you to lay off Ronan and friends. I take it the 'people in the neighbourhood' is them," Elwyn said.

"I only want a chat, Elwyn, get a handle on what they're up to. I've got a sneaky feeling that the dealing going on around here is a lot more serious than we first thought. Otherwise, why would the drugs squad be that interested? And I'm betting it has something to do with Jacob Gilbert. Somewhere in all this mess is a link to Neville, and the reason why Mary was murdered."

"That's a bit of a leap," he said. "We have no proof that Neville has anything to do with the dealing. And Gilbert had nothing to do with the Slasher killings."

"But he was married to the Slasher's sister."

CHAPTER SEVENTEEN

Back at the station, Kenton wanted to know why the church was getting so much attention. "I've had the bishop on the phone — now there's a first," he said sardonically.

"Mary Dunn's flat has been gone over," Rachel said. "It looks very much like the person who did it was looking for something. Given that the church was practically her second home — well it doesn't take much figuring out. We've applied for a warrant and will make a start in the morning."

"She was an ageing pensioner, for goodness' sake. What could she possibly have had that would cause so much interest in the criminal fraternity?"

"It could have been anything, sir. We know about the dealing that's been going on, perhaps she found someone's stash."

Kenton shook his head. "You're barking up the wrong tree, Rachel. And even if you're not, my instructions were to leave that aspect of it to the drugs squad."

"Over the years that church has had some interesting people attending services such as weddings and funerals," she explained. "The Gilberts, to name only two, and Tara Shepherd's son. Tara was Lauren Gilbert's sister. Given the Slasher connection, it is quite possible that I will soon have to speak to all the members of that family. In my opinion, a conversation with Jacob Gilbert is much more dangerous than searching a church."

Kenton looked decidedly unhappy. "I don't recommend speaking to any of that lot, Rachel. Not given your own rather dubious connections."

She shot him a look. "What's that supposed to mean?"

"You know very well what I mean. You were living with Jed McAteer for a while. You were a couple and have a child together. That is not a recipe for getting the best out of a man like Jacob Gilbert. Make no mistake, he'll know who you are and if he can use it against you, he will."

"That's a chance I'll just have to take," she said.

"Just a friendly warning, Rachel. The two men were rivals. At one point Gilbert had a price on McAteer's head. Things only calmed down after Grace Blackmore had a word."

Rachel had known none of this. Jed had never even mentioned Gilbert. "Nonetheless, sir, if any member of that family is implicated, I will speak to them."

"Well, don't do anything without telling me first, so I can arrange backup. I mean that, Rachel. Do you understand?"

She nodded. "The search of the church, sir. Can I go ahead?"

"I suppose so, since you're so determined, though I can't for the life of me think what you expect to find there."

* * *

Back in the main office, Jonny and Amy were hard at it. Jonny was researching Tara and Lauren Lawson's background, while Amy examined the Slasher's victims for any link with Mary. Neither had found anything of particular interest yet.

"Message from Superintendent Sharpe, ma'am," Amy said. "He can see you at his station on Friday morning."

Fair enough. She had plenty on for now. "Tomorrow morning we're searching the church," Rachel told them. She looked at Elwyn. "See if you can find plans of the place. That building is old with any number of hidey holes. We don't want to miss any."

"What're we looking for, ma'am?" Amy asked.

"I've no idea," Rachel said. "But whatever it is, I have a horrible feeling it's what got poor Mary killed.

"Elwyn, have Uniform watch the place tonight. I want someone in that graveyard and another officer inside. They see anyone that looks even vaguely like they're dealing and they bring them in."

Elwyn looked doubtful.

"Come on then, out with it."

He jerked his thumb. "Your office."

"If you're trying to spare my blushes in front of the others, don't bother. I'm a big girl now."

"We're working blind, Rachel," he said. "The truth is, we have no idea why Mary was murdered, but I strongly doubt it has anything to do with something she hid."

"Well, I strongly doubt she was a random," Rachel retorted.

"Then there's all the Slasher stuff. How d'you explain that?" Elwyn said.

"I can't right now. All I can do, Elwyn, is go with my gut, and it's telling me to tear that church apart if we have to."

* * *

Rachel decided on an early finish. She had a feeling tomorrow would be a big day. Besides, she was anxious to find out how Sofia had got on with the kids. Despite the glowing references and Belinda's recommendation, leaving them with a stranger was a big deal and, ordinarily, not something she would even consider. But with luck, Sofia would get used to them and they her.

The first thing that hit Rachel as she entered the house was the wonderful aroma wafting from the kitchen.

"It's some sort of stew her mother used to make," Mia said, making for the stairs. "We eat at six and then I'm off round to Chloe's."

Very organised. "Everything okay?" Rachel whispered.

"Yeah, great. Sofia even helped me with my homework. She's a wiz at algebra."

"And Len?"

"He's fine, he's in his playpen with that car he likes so much."

Rachel went into the kitchen. Sofia was laying the table, humming quietly to herself.

She smiled at Rachel. "I hope you like what I've made. It is a favourite at home and always makes me feel happy."

"Any problems?"

"No, everything has been great. Belinda went home mid-afternoon and we guys have been getting to know each other. Len is no trouble."

"Your room okay?"

"It's perfect and I love it," Sofia said. "It is so kind of you to give me this opportunity."

"It works both ways. You are doing me a huge favour too," Rachel said. "Without help I couldn't continue to work."

"You are police, aren't you? A detective, so Belinda tells me."

"Yes, and my job is full on, I'm afraid."

"You need not worry about this end anymore. I have everything in hand."

"You haven't always lived in the north of England, have you?" Rachel said.

"No. My father was in the army. When I was younger, we spent quite a lot of time abroad. My accent is a bit rogue, I'm afraid."

Rachel smiled at her. So far, so good.

CHAPTER EIGHTEEN

Thursday

The following morning, the CID team plus a number of uniformed officers gathered at the church. Elwyn handed out copies of the plans and gave everyone a specific area to look at.

"The building is nearly two hundred years old, so it might not be exactly as laid out in the plan, so use your initiative," Elwyn said.

Rachel studied the drawing closely. "Who gave you this?"

"The vicar," Elwyn said. "We needed to know the layout before going in, and he was the best person to ask."

But Rachel wasn't so sure. If he was party to this, and knew that something had been hidden, he would be holding back. There could be places not shown on the plan. "I want you to give this place a thorough going over from top to bottom," she told the assembled officers. "Look in every room, every drawer and cupboard."

"Even the bell tower?" one of the uniforms asked. "Only it might not be that easy to get up there."

He was right, and clambering up into the roof space could pose a health and safety issue. "Leave the tower till last," Rachel said. "If we find nothing anywhere else, we'll look at getting professional help."

At that moment Henry Neville appeared, with a man in tow who he introduced as his brother, George. "I'm not the tidiest person" he said. "Your task won't be easy, I'm afraid, and you're going to find all sorts — old paperwork, artefacts, the lot."

"I can vouch for that," George Neville added. "That back room is full of stuff for the weekend jumble sale. My dear brother here has given me the job of sorting it out."

"This place is bigger than it looks," Jonny Farrell said, approaching them with a large cardboard box in his arms. "That back room, for instance. Apart from all the junk on the floor, it's lined with cupboards, and each one is stuffed with all sorts. There's paperwork going back decades."

Rachel stuck her hand in the box and pulled out a sheaf of papers. Jonny was right. There were orders of service and printed hymn sheets here from years ago. Jonny gave a loud sneeze as if to emphasise his point.

"This is no good," Rachel said. "We could be here all week and not find anything."

"It would help, ma'am, if we knew what we were looking for," Jonny said. "I know you're convinced there's something here, but we'll never find it like this." Jonny sneezed again. "Dust always gets to me." He pulled a hankie from his jacket pocket, bringing a number of coins with it. They fell to the floor and rolled in all directions.

Rachel crouched down to help retrieve them. "Where did that fifty pence piece go?" The floor was made up of flat stone slabs and the coin had dropped in a wide crack between two of them. She pulled the plan from her pocket. It gave no indication of there being anything below ground level.

"Elwyn, I think there's a cellar," she called out. She looked up to ask Neville about it, but both he and his brother had disappeared.

"It's called a crypt, Rachel," Elwyn said. "And you could be right, although it's not on the plan."

"Something the good reverend didn't want us to know about, I wonder?" She turned to Jonny. "Go and find him. I'd like a word."

"Finding the entrance to the crypt could be a problem. I've been all over this building and haven't found a likely door or stairs," Elwyn said.

"Hidden behind a large piece of furniture, d'you reckon?" Rachel took a walk down the aisle towards the back room. "Check anything large set against a wall."

"How can I help?" Henry Neville came up to join them.

Rachel looked him in the eye. "You can tell us how to get into the crypt. You appear to have left it off your plan of the building."

"Crypt?" he echoed. "But no one's been down there in years. Are you sure it's really necessary to search it?"

"Just show one of my officers how to access it and we'll decide whether it's necessary."

"I really wouldn't go down there," Neville said. "It's a dangerous place, cold and dirty, with steep stone steps. There's no daylight or fresh air down there."

"All the more reason to take a look," she said. "We wouldn't have found it if it hadn't been for one of my officers dropping a coin from his pocket that fell down a crack in the floor."

With a look of resignation, Neville led them into the back room and pointed out a large bookshelf. "The door is behind here. Be sure to put all the books back as you found them. And you should know that the crypt is the final resting place of a number of long dead incumbents of this parish."

Rachel couldn't help shuddering. "What d'you mean? Are there bodies down there?"

"Caskets, possibly, in one of the back rooms. Plus, a number of urns containing ashes."

Unpalatable as it was, Rachel still considered the search to be necessary. Gritting her teeth, she called to the team. "Right, let's get this done."

"D'you really think Mary saw something going on in the crypt?" Elwyn asked. "I don't see how she could."

"We take a look, Elwyn. If we find nothing, then fair enough, we'll chalk it up to my rusty skills, but I think Neville is being far too shifty. I want to know why he left this crypt off his plan for a start."

It took them nearly an hour to remove the books and shift the heavy oak bookshelf. The door behind it was narrow. It was also locked.

Rachel looked round for Neville. "We need the key. Go and find the vicar," she told Amy.

The team and Rachel waited impatiently. Rachel grew increasingly certain they had something. After several minutes, Amy returned, shaking her head.

"He's gone. I heard him driving off as I walked across his garden."

"Were there any keys lying around?"

"He has a set of hooks in the kitchen but, if there were keys on them, they aren't there now, ma'am."

"He's done a runner." Rachel looked at Elwyn. "The only reason I can see for him going off like that is because he's afraid of what we'll find down there." She looked round at the group of uniformed officers. "Get an axe or something and break the lock. I want access to the crypt now."

CHAPTER NINETEEN

Elwyn, torch in hand, led the way down the stone stairs with Rachel close behind. "Did anyone see a light switch?" she called back, flashing her own torch at the space opening up in front of them.

"Found it," Jonny called.

The low wattage single bulb hanging from the high ceiling was hardly adequate to illuminate the large area. Rachel reached out and felt the stone wall to her side. She wanted something to hold onto other than Elwyn's arm, but there was no rail. Running her hand against the rough, hard surface she found it dirty and covered in cobwebs. The vicar was right, the crypt was little used. She shone her torch beam into every corner. Dust motes floated in the light, and the team were all coughing and sneezing.

"This is creepy," she whispered to Elwyn. "You're right, I can't see Mary coming down here." She looked back at the others. "Tread carefully now. One of you get back up there and organise some proper lighting."

Elwyn helped her down the last few steps and shone his torch on them, for Jonny and Amy. "I agree. Those steps are far too dangerous for a woman of her age. We've got quite a task on. This is a big area and it's going to take some searching."

Rachel was beginning to doubt her own instincts. Was this the wrong move? She decided to reserve judgement until she'd had a look around. "Seeing as we've come this far, we'll give it our best shot. Search in pairs, the crypt is far bigger than I'd expected and I don't want anyone getting lost."

She was right about the size. The crypt was divided into four areas, each with a vaulted ceiling and stone walls and floors.

Rachel followed in Elwyn's wake as, tentatively, he made his way around the perimeter of the largest room. "There's an odd smell," she said. "What d'you think?"

"Decades of decay probably. The vicars of the church have been dumping unwanted stuff here for years."

It was more than that. "Unwanted stuff and the ashes of previous colleagues. Makes me cringe just thinking about it."

"We'll have a quick look and if anything strikes us as suspicious, go from there," Elwyn said.

Sensible, but Rachel was still sure that what they were looking for was here. Who knew what could have been hidden in this dark chamber through the decades and no one any the wiser. The pair passed through a stone archway into a smaller area. The only lighting here was that from their torches and what little filtered in from the larger room. Elwyn flashed the strong beam of his torch around the walls and the floor.

"What's that?" Rachel pointed. "In the far corner. There's what looks like a bundle."

Elwyn led the way across. "Old clothing, I expect."

But as they got closer, it became obvious that this was not discarded clothing. There was an iron ring fastened into the stone wall, and chained to it, a pale, bony hand. Rachel stifled a scream. She knew in that moment that her instincts had been right. This had to be the reason Mary Dunn was murdered, although it was anyone's guess what her connection with this poor individual had been.

"It's a body, Elwyn," Rachel gasped. "The poor sod's been chained up and left down here."

Elwyn dragged what appeared to be a tarpaulin away from the body. One of the bones was sticking out of the arm. This poor soul had suffered prior to death. The body was clothed and appeared to have been reasonably preserved. She'd not been dead long then, he decided. "It looks like the body of a young girl," he said. "I'd say she's not been down here long. I'd say not long, days rather than weeks."

Feeling sick, Rachel took a closer look. The poor lass had been tortured. "As well as the broken arm some of her fingernails on the unchained hand are missing, perhaps the other one too, but it's difficult to tell because of bad light."

"Whoever did this wanted something from her," Elwyn whispered. "God knows what, but it must have been important to them."

"We need Butterworth and Jude," Rachel said. "In fact, we need a whole bloody forensic team down here, and a lot more light."

Jonny and Amy came up behind them. Amy took one look and let out an involuntary shriek. After a couple of seconds, she was able to ask, "How long?"

Rachel looked at the young woman. Good question. From the way she was dressed and the state of the body, Elwyn could be right and she'd been put here recently.

"There's bloodstains on the floor. If I had to guess I'd say she was shot, but I wonder how long she was left a prisoner down here before that happened?" Elwyn said.

Rachel didn't want to think about that one. She hoped it hadn't been too long. She could think of nothing worse than to be abandoned down here in the cold, the dark and in pain, with no hope of rescue. It was one of the cruellest ways to die. The bullet that finished her off might have come as a blessed relief.

CHAPTER TWENTY

Dr Colin Butterworth looked up from the body. "She was shot through the heart. There's a pool of blood on the floor under her body and an exit wound in her back."

"And the torture? Did she suffer much?" Rachel hoped he'd say not but he gave a little nod.

"It looks that way, the nails for one, and I found a number of burns on her legs and arms," he said.

Rachel sighed. Poor girl. Who had she crossed to bring this on herself?

"Estimating her age is tricky,' Dr Butterworth said, "but I did take a quick look inside her mouth and her wisdom teeth were still in the process of erupting."

Young then. It brought an unexpected tear to Rachel's eye. Whatever she'd done, the girl didn't deserve this.

"Her clothing suggests she's young too," Jude added, indicating the short skirt and denim jacket.

"Anything that might help us identify her?" Rachel asked.

"I've made a cursory search but there's no mobile or bag and nothing in her pockets. Though we may get something on closer examination back at the lab," Jude said.

"I want Henry Neville finding and bringing in for questioning," Rachel told Jonny. "Get a photo, description and details of his car circulated."

"You reckon he knew?" Amy asked.

"Of course, he did, that's what all the reluctance to help has been about. As well as his eagerness to put the blame for Mary's murder on Ronan Dunn."

"In what way d'you think Mary's death is connected to this girl?" Elwyn asked.

"I think she found out or saw something. If she did, it would have made her a potential danger. And I'll stake my pension on Neville knowing exactly what happened, as well as Mary's part in it."

"We'll conduct a full forensic search, take samples. You know the drill," Jude said.

"Finding the bullet might be helpful. With any luck it's buried in the wall behind her," Rachel said.

"Rest assured, we'll look for it," Jude said.

"We'll get her out of here," Butterworth said. "But I'll need someone to prise that ring from the wall."

"We'll take it with us," Jude explained. "There may be prints or DNA on it from the sadist who left her here."

"I'm thinking that they didn't expect her to be found, so they might not have been too careful," Rachel said.

"Let's hope you're right," Jude said.

You could say the morning had been a success. The find was sad and gruesome but it was another piece of the puzzle.

"Amy, when we return to the station, see if our girl is listed as missing. She's young, someone must be wondering what's happened to her."

"She could have been a rough sleeper, ma'am," Jonny said. "Manchester has its fair share of them. If Jude can do me a reasonable photo, I'll ask around."

Jonny volunteered at the homeless shelter on Oldham Road whenever he could. Even though they knew he was police, the people who used it trusted him and had helped him in the past.

"It's a good idea, but her clothing doesn't shout homeless to me. Let Jude have a closer look at the labels, see where it was bought, and we'll go from there."

"A runaway then. Perhaps she took shelter in the church. She could have got mixed up with the drug runners around here and ended up dead," Jonny said.

Sounded like a neat explanation but Rachel suspected that wasn't what had happened at all. The dealing was a side issue, unrelated to what they were looking at. This case was about something else entirely.

* * *

Back outside, Rachel stood still for a moment and inhaled deeply. It was still relatively early in the morning and the air was fresh and sweet. She was shaking. The dead girl had been young, of a similar age to her two daughters. Rachel told herself to get a grip. Thinking this way would not do her any good at all.

"So, it looks as if Mary was killed because of something she saw, not something she hid," Elwyn said, coming up to stand beside her.

"We were both right after a fashion. Mary's involvement with this church and Henry Neville is what got her killed."

"What about the Lawson aspect?" Elwyn asked. "We can't ignore forensic evidence."

"The hair could have been placed there deliberately to confuse us," Rachel said. "It's the only explanation that makes any sense."

"Okay, say we go with that. That means that whoever killed Mary must have had some of Lawson's hair. I'd imagine that would rule out everyone except close friends or family members."

It was something to chew over. Though after the experience she'd just had, Rachel certainly didn't fancy topping it off by chatting to Lawson's sister, Lauren Gilbert, about her murdering brother.

"I'm seeing a detective in the morning who worked the Slasher case. I'll tell him what we've found and get his take on it," Rachel told him.

"Which detective?"

"A Detective Superintendent Hedley Sharpe. D'you know him?"

"No, but I've heard rumours. Big bloke, blunt, tells it like it is and doesn't suffer fools." Elwyn grinned. "I'm sure the pair of you will hit it off just fine."

CHAPTER TWENTY-ONE

Back at the station, Rachel brought Kenton up to speed with events. "A young girl, chained to a wall, tortured and then shot dead. Had we not gone into that crypt she may never have been found. I've put out a call for Neville, who took off during the search. Seems to me he knew damn well what was there."

"You're jumping to conclusions, Rachel. The man is afraid. You went in there mob-handed, determined to find something. I doubt he's run, it's more likely he's absented himself until it's all over."

Rachel did not understand Kenton's attitude. It was plain enough to her. Neville knew more than he'd told them, and she wanted to know what that was.

"What's your next move?" Kenton asked.

"We're awaiting the PM but before that can happen I need to find her family, give the girl a name."

"Okay, keep me in the loop."

Rachel left his office and returned to the incident room. "Amy, you and Jonny carry on looking at missing persons, see if any of them could be our victim."

"I've been thinking," Elwyn said. "Given that Mary was best friends with Dotty, I can't believe that if she knew there was a body in that crypt she wouldn't have confided in her."

"So why hasn't Dotty said anything then?" Rachel said. "We've given the woman every opportunity to tell us what she knows."

Elwyn smiled. "We hadn't found the body then. Perhaps Dotty is afraid too. We should speak to her and the others again, tell them what's happened."

Rachel checked the time. "Midday. Okay, give me a minute to speak to Jude, and ask if she's likely to have anything for us today. If she doesn't think there will be, we'll go and have that word with Dotty and the others."

"I was just going to call you," Jude said after Rachel put a call through to her. "Running tests takes time, but while we wait, I have got something. We found a photo in one of her jacket pockets. Fortunately, it hasn't got too much blood on it. It's of our victim, and she's with a man, but only half of him is in the picture. I don't reckon we've got enough to identify him, though."

"Text me over the image and I'll pass it to the team."

"Meanwhile I'll continue with the blood and other tests so we will have something for you by this time tomorrow."

That left the afternoon free to speak to Mary's friends again. Back in the incident room, Rachel gestured to Elwyn. "Dotty and co it is then. This time we push hard, see what gives. I can't believe that Mary saw what was going on and didn't tell Dotty at least."

* * *

Dotty was surprised to see the two detectives at her door again. "Is something wrong?" she asked anxiously. "Only I'm about to leave for the bingo session at the community hall."

"We've found something," Rachel said. "I suspect it might be the reason why Mary was murdered."

"What d'you mean? What have you found?" Dotty looked frightened.

"Are you sure Mary didn't confide in you? Perhaps she told you something so dreadful you've put it to the back of your mind."

Dotty wiped a stray tear from her eye. "There is something but . . . I'm not sure. It's been such a dreadful time I can't remember the details exactly."

"Sit down, Dotty," Elwyn said, leading her to a chair. "I'm afraid we've found the body of a young girl in the church crypt. Rachel here and I both think that Mary might have seen or heard something which made the killer see her as a threat."

"I don't understand . . ." Dotty looked from one detective to the other. "Mary said the body would never be found. She was positive about that, she said no one ever went down there."

"She did tell you about her then," Rachel said.

Dotty nodded. "She told all of us. We discussed it in the communal lounge one night. Mary was distraught. She wanted to tell the police but Reg said it was best to say nothing. He said it put us all in danger, that the killer would want to make sure she and the rest of us kept quiet." Dotty looked up at them, her eyes full of tears. "He must have seen her because he contacted her and threatened her. She was terrified. He told her that if she said anything, got the police involved, he would kill Kimberley and Ronan before killing her."

Rachel took Elwyn to one side. "Go and see if Reg Hitchin is in. I think we should have a word."

"Did Mary know who the girl was?" she asked.

Dotty shook her head. "She was doing the flowers one night when she heard screaming and shouting coming from the crypt. The girl and an older man she said. She was relieved when all went quiet but then she heard the gunshot."

"Did she know the man?" Rachel asked.

"She said not, but I didn't believe her. I think she wouldn't tell me or the others to keep us safe. All she said was that the girl was young, a pretty little thing with black hair."

"Are you sure Mary said nothing about the killer, the smallest thing would help at this point."

Dotty shook her head. "She did say there were two of them and they wore masks with hoods pulled down over their heads. But she did recognise the voice of one of them. Apparently, she called out his name." Dotty shook her head. "She didn't tell me what that name was, just that she'd spoken it out loud." Dotty fell silent for a moment. "I reckon that's what got her killed."

"Two of them, you said. She was sure?" Rachel asked.

Dotty nodded. She gave them a bit more of the story but nothing that really helped. Soon, Elwyn was back with Reg in tow.

"I'm glad to see you're out of hospital," Rachel said.

"Thank you. Look, I'm sorry about the secrecy. All I wanted was to keep Mary and her family safe. You see, two days after the girl was killed, a man, one of the killers, I presume, rang Mary." Reg nodded at Dotty. "Go on. Tell them."

"He said that her grandson, Ronan, was involved." Dotty looked at the two detectives. "We had no idea if he was or not, but Mary wouldn't take the risk. We wanted to come to you, give a statement and tell the truth, but how could we? The killer said he'd kill her family if news of the killing got out. Mary had to protect them and if that meant keeping quiet about the girl, then so be it."

"Did she have proof that Ronan was involved?"

Dotty shook her head. "She didn't say in so many words, but I got the impression she knew more about the murder than she told us. Like I said, she recognised one of them from their voice. She was very upset, I know that. And she was worried about the company Ronan was keeping. A rough bunch is what she said."

"It was a worrying few days, I can tell you," Reg said. "That young girl who got killed must have been mixed up with some dangerous types. We all feel for her, we really do, but at our age we can do without the aggro."

"Aggro!" Rachel exclaimed. "Both the girl and Mary lost their lives! She should have come to us straight away, and after she was killed, you definitely should. I don't understand why you all held back."

"Mary thought she could protect them both."

Rachel stared at Reg. "Why would she think that? Any idea?"

"Because Mary had insurance," Reg piped up. "She found something in the crypt, something that had been left with the girl's body. She brought it here and we hid it."

Rachel was amazed that a woman of Mary's age could have negotiated those stone stairs and found her way around in the darkness. "Mary went down into the crypt?"

"She told us that she had to find out what had happened to the girl. The poor thing was dead and in a dreadful state. Mary got quite a shock, I know that."

"This thing she found, this insurance, what happened to it?" Elwyn asked.

Reg looked at Dotty and nodded.

"We wrapped it in a plastic bag," she said, "and buried it in that raised vegetable bed over there, next to the bird table."

Rachel looked at the pair and then at Elwyn. "Exactly what is it, this insurance?"

With a glance at Dotty, Reg said, "Something that may yield evidence you can use. The gun the young lass was shot with."

Rachel was amazed. These retirees were fearless, it seemed. "How did Mary find it? Didn't the killer hide it?"

"Yes, he did," Reg confirmed. "Mary told us that she heard one of them tell the other that he'd put it in an urn close to her body. He must have tipped out the ashes and put the gun inside. I mean, who would think to look for a gun somewhere like that?"

CHAPTER TWENTY-TWO

With the plastic bag — retrieved by Elwyn and in the boot of his car — the pair drove to Jude's lab to hand it over. It was likely that Reg was right, and it would yield DNA or prints. It could be the break they needed. The big question: why had the killer left it behind? It was an odd thing to do. The only answer Rachel could come up with was that the killer was certain that no one was likely to go down to the crypt and find it, especially not in an urn full of ashes. Perhaps he intended to return for it when he was sure the heat had died down.

"So, where does the young girl fit into it all?" Elwyn asked.

"Your guess is as good as mine. Maybe she was someone Neville knew, or Ronan and his mate, Arlo. Regardless of the drug squad's objections, we need a word with them both."

Rachel took her mobile from her pocket and checked the photo Jude had sent her. It showed a smiling teenager with long dark hair. Next to her was a man, but half of him had been cut off. Rachel wondered if this was an attempt to hide his identity.

"This girl, our victim, she reminds me of someone," she told Elwyn.

But Elwyn wasn't listening. He was muttering angrily to himself. "If Mary had spoken up, if she'd only said something to us, we would have protected her. I despair sometimes, I really do."

"Well at least now we know why Mary got herself killed, though it hasn't helped our workload any," Rachel said.

"And what about the Slasher connection?" he said. "The young girl was shot, not his style at all."

"I told you, Elwyn, the Slasher is long dead. Someone is playing games with us, trying to muddy the waters."

He grunted. "Not doing a bad job of it either."

They pulled into the lab car park. "Keep your fingers crossed that Jude's found something for us from her search of the crypt," Rachel said hopefully.

"It seems to me that the killers worked on the theory that no one would venture down there," Elwyn said. "A bit ambitious if you ask me. Sooner or later, that space was bound to be disturbed."

"Perhaps they were counting on it being years before that happened. And the body was in the far room and not easily visible. Even so, it was a bit of an amateur job, wasn't it?"

"Wonder who the poor girl upset," Elwyn said. "The drug dealers? The likes of Mary's grandson? Killing her like that seems a bit extreme to be the result of an argument with a couple of teenage boys."

* * *

"What delights have you got for me now?" Jude nodded at the package Elwyn was holding.

"We strongly suspect that this is the gun that killed the girl in the crypt," he said.

She smiled. "Nice work. For our part, we've retrieved several cigarette ends and an empty beer can. We'll process the lot for DNA. I'm hoping to have the initial results tomorrow."

"It appears Mary was killed because she witnessed the young girl's murder. She may even have known the killers, but we're not sure about that."

"Colin might want us to find a relative to identify her before he does the PM, but meanwhile, I've had a look at her clothing. It was expensive, designer stuff. However, everything was the wrong size for her. That denim jacket she was wearing was too big, and she'd rolled up the waistband of the skirt. They hadn't been washed in a while either. I doubt they were hers originally which means she'd possibly been living rough."

Rachel sighed. "Poor thing. What a life. To have to live on your wits on the streets and then end up dead in a church crypt." Rachel felt this one keenly. Their victim could well be the same age as her daughter, Megan. She gathered herself. "Right then, we'll leave you with the gun. Tell Colin I'll contact him tomorrow about the PM, but Elwyn might have to attend on his own. I've got a meeting with a detective from Old Trafford, one Hedley Sharpe. Know him?"

"Oh yes, he's quite a character is Hedley. Good at his job though. Doesn't miss much. An old-fashioned results copper, well thought of among his colleagues, even though he can be a pain in the butt. No family, you see." Jude winked. "Means he can work all hours and often expects the same from his team."

Useful info. "Right then. We'll be in touch tomorrow."

Once outside Rachel asked to be dropped off at the station so she could pick up her car and leave for home. Although Sofia was settling in nicely, she still felt the need to keep an eye on things.

"I'll pick up the file and have a read through later at home," she told Elwyn. "Homework for my meeting with Superintendent Sharpe tomorrow. From the description Jude gave us, he sounds formidable, and I don't want to be caught without the facts at my fingertips."

CHAPTER TWENTY-THREE

Friday

The Old Trafford station was a modern two-storey building. Given they were both in the serious crime squad, Rachel wondered why Hedley Sharpe had been shifted out of the city centre. It smacked of him having a story to tell; sadly, she had no time to hear it today.

Rachel checked in at the main desk and a DC Robert Payne came down to greet her. "Superintendent Sharpe's office is on the second floor. He likes the view over the city."

Knowing nothing about the man, Rachel didn't know what to say to this. "Have you worked with him long?"

"Six months — and believe me, he takes some getting used to," Payne said, confirming Rachel's fears that involving Hedley Sharpe might turn out to be more bothersome than it was worth. "He's a real stickler for getting the detail exactly right and doesn't tolerate cutting corners."

They were only a few steps away from Sharpe's office door when she heard the thick, Lancashire accent resonate down the corridor. He sounded distinctly annoyed. "I told you to get out there and bring him in. Stop pissing about and do as you're told."

A tall, slim man, his eyes wide, exited the office hurriedly as Rachel readied herself to enter the lion's den.

"Not one ounce of gumption, a face like a wet Whit Friday and he wonders why I shout. Bloody university types. Whatever happened to real policing? It takes hard men to do this job, I tell them upstairs, but do they listen?"

For several seconds he subjected Rachel to an unflinching stare. No doubt he was taking in every detail. If he thought the new boys were wimps, what did he think of women detectives?

"This evidence you've found," he said, pointing to a chair. "The rose, the body left on the altar and the rest, it's nowt but a bloody wind-up. Some funny bugger's making you work hard for his own amusement."

"My team are simply following leads, sir."

"Leads that take you nowhere," he scoffed. "This bugger's having a laugh at your expense, love. Lawson's dead, he's not rampaging around Ancoats killing people, not anymore."

"We have a body, murdered and left in a certain way, a way that matches the Slasher's MO."

Sharpe dismissed this with a wave of his hand. "The details are easy enough to get hold of. What you have is a copycat, nowt else."

Rachel gritted her teeth. This man was so sure, so positive that he was right, and it irritated her. He left no room for any other conclusion. "There is other evidence, Superintendent Sharpe."

"Call me Hedley, Rachel," he said. "As long as the job gets done I'm not big on protocol. What evidence?" he asked.

"Our first murder victim had Lawson's hair on her coat. He attacked her from behind and we reckon that she reached back, grabbed his hair and some was left on the collar," Rachel said.

"Hair, you say. Definitely Lawson's, was it?"

"Yes, sir, DNA confirms it to be so."

Sharpe gazed at her thoughtfully for a few moments. "I can see your problem but perhaps I can help you there too.

Before you get too entrenched in the notion that your killer is the Slasher, let me tell you a little story."

Was he taking the piss? Rachel couldn't be sure. She waited with some scepticism for the 'story'.

He cleared his throat. "Once upon a time there was a killer called John Lawson, alias the 'Ancoats Slasher'. But you know that. Wicked and unrepentant as he was, the only people he was close to, who he loved and who loved him back, were his two sisters, Tara and Lauren. In their eyes he could do no wrong and they would hear nothing bad said against him. The pair kept a close eye on big brother but one of them, Lauren, watched to the point of obsession."

"Obsession? In what way?" Rachel asked.

"She kept his favourite toys from childhood, some of his clothing from when he was a baby. During a search we made of her home following a robbery, she told us that, apart from money and jewellery, a lock of Lawson's hair that she kept in a small silk bag was missing from the safe. She'd intended to have it made up into a piece of mourning jewellery but hadn't got round to it."

"What you're saying is that whoever committed this robbery took a lock of Lawson's hair and deliberately left it at our crime scene to . . . muddy the waters, as you put it."

"Exactly that, love. We can't be sure whether or not they realised its significance at the time, but I suspect they did, and that narrows the field."

"In what way?"

"In my book there is only one person who would realise that that hair could come in useful, who knew who it belonged to and its significance. You see, Lauren is Lauren Gilbert. You'll be aware of their reputation of course."

"I still don't see. Who are you talking about?"

"Have you heard of an individual known only as 'Ghost'?"

Rachel shook her head.

"Ghost is a villain who's been active in the Manchester underworld in recent times and is known to the Gilberts.

The two men are sworn enemies, although I've never been able to find out what happened between them to make them hate each other so."

"You think that this Ghost murdered Mary Dunn and made it look as if the killer was Lauren Gilbert's brother, the Slasher? Why would he do that? Why go to all the bother? He must know that Lawson is long dead."

"I've no idea, but I bet it threw the investigation for a short while, and that may have been crucial in some way," he said.

"We found Mary Dunn's body in the church done up like one of the Slasher's victims, but in the crypt we found another body — that of a young girl. She'd been held captive, beaten and finally shot dead."

"That sounds like Gilbert's MO. The man has no heart. He has no feelings whatsoever and is able to kill without the slightest compunction. Jacob Gilbert is responsible for bringing trafficked individuals into the city and selling them on to whoever will pay his price. Perhaps your young girl is one who became troublesome."

"Tell me about this robbery when the hair was taken."

"A trafficked girl they recently had working as Lauren's maid took several items from the safe one night when Lauren mistakenly left it open. Mostly jewels, according to the lovely Lauren, but I suspect she was lying. I know from information we gathered that most of the Gilberts' wealth — money, jewels and the like — is kept in a safety deposit box in the bank. I'll lay odds that the missing package contained drugs, most likely heroin. Plus the lock of hair she listed on the missing items."

All very interesting but still not what Rachel wanted to know. "What happened to the girl?"

"We've no idea, she disappeared onto Manchester's streets and hasn't surfaced since."

"It's possible that Gilbert did catch up with her and that she is our body in the crypt. The church is known to Lauren Gilbert," Rachel said.

Hedley shrugged. "Might be if Gilbert caught up with her, she'd surely end up dead in that case. But as for the murder of the old woman, like I said, some bugger's playing games and that isn't Gilbert's style. My advice is to look elsewhere for whoever is behind that one. But take my word for it, Lawson didn't kill either of your victims." Sharpe picked up a file from his desk. "Take this with you and return it when you're done. It's observations I've made over the years about the Gilberts and Jacob's arch enemy, Ghost. It makes interesting reading and might be of help."

"But why Ghost?" Rachel asked.

"Because no one knows who the bugger is. No one recalls even seeing him," he said.

"Thanks, Hedley, much appreciated. If ever I can help you with anything, just let me know," Rachel said, getting to her feet.

"Just be careful, love. Gilbert's certainly someone to be wary of, but rumour has it that there's a new boy on the local scene who's out to make a name for himself."

"D'you know what he's called? Any more information about him?"

"Just that he's young, ambitious, a hard man and eager to oust Gilbert." Hedley smiled. "That villain is getting on in years and should have retired long ago. Most of his old guard have gone and left him to it. If someone is looking to stage a takeover, then their timing's perfect." He looked at her long and hard. "That puts Gilbert on his mettle and makes him dangerous, and he's not stupid either."

Not Gilbert, someone new. This gave Rachel plenty to think about. "Do you mean he's this Ghost?"

Hedley gave her a big grin. "Could be anyone, love. There's plenty of wasters on the streets these days. Mind you, you're looking for a waster with a brain. As for Ghost, he's been around a long time too and I believe his only interest is in making Gilbert pay for some past misdemeanour or other."

Rachel was going through the people involved in the case so far, but none of them really fitted the bill.

"Speaking of wasters, how's that idiot Kenton getting on these days?" Hedley suddenly said.

The question and the way Hedley had asked it took Rachel by surprise. "Er, he's fine." She wasn't sure how to take the question, or how to respond. Was Hedley a friend of Kenton's and merely joking?

But it seemed he was serious. "Watch him. Take it from one who knows. If it means dropping you in it to save himself then that's what he'll do. I know the bastard of old."

She wondered what the history was between the pair. "I've always found him okay."

"Until things go pear-shaped, and then watch out. Kenton's all about saving his own skin and to hell with everyone else." He gave Rachel a nod. "Why d'you think I moved out here? Take my advice and remember it."

CHAPTER TWENTY-FOUR

Rachel returned to her office and found several messages on her desk. One, marked urgent, was from Jude.

Rachel called her at once. "Hi, what've you got?"

"I've had a look at all the objects brought in so far and can find no trace of Jack Fairhurst's DNA."

Rachel heaved a sigh of relief. Kimberley Dunn, Mary's daughter, had suffered enough. To find out at this point that her boyfriend had betrayed her and was involved in her mother's murder would have finished her. "Anything else?" she asked.

"We're still processing the gun and the plastic bag. The gun, however, has 'Ghost' inscribed on the barrel. Any idea what that means, if anything?"

Remembering what Hedley Sharpe had said, Rachel chose to ignore the question. It was too complicated to explain right now. 'D'you think you'll get much from the bag it was found in?"

"Well, it's covered in prints, but it's the usual supermarket issue, so it could have been hanging around in someone's kitchen drawer for weeks. But don't worry, it'll get the full treatment."

"Thanks, Jude. Any idea about the post-mortem?"

"Ideally Colin would like her identity clarifying. If, as you suspect, she ran away from the Gilbert household, you may have to approach him."

Rachel hoped it wouldn't come to that. Approaching Gilbert about anything was way down her to-do list right now. "Okay, we will if we have to, but we'll do our best to find an alternative. The girl does have a mother somewhere."

Call over, she went into the main office to catch up with the team. "Never mind the drug squad, I want Arlo Bain finding and bringing in," she told them. "Tell Uniform to keep an eye out for him." She turned to Jonny. "Anything on the young girl who scarpered from the Gilbert house?"

"Not yet, ma'am, but I'll be out there tonight so I'll have another try."

"Has Henry Neville turned up yet?"

Amy said, "We went back to the church but only his brother was there. He maintained he'd no idea where the vicar had gone. Then we had a bit of luck. Neville was pulled over for speeding on the M62, heading towards Leeds. I'm having him brought back." She checked the clock on the wall. "He should be here any time now, I reckon."

Rachel smiled. "Well done, Amy. Want to join me for the interview when he arrives?"

Amy looked delighted, as if she could hardly believe her luck.

"Yes, ma'am, I'd like that."

* * *

In less than an hour, Reverend Henry Neville had been processed and was sitting in an interview room.

"I don't understand," he began as soon as Rachel and Amy walked in. "I've done nothing wrong."

Ignoring him, Rachel introduced those present for the recording. Neville had requested the duty solicitor, a man called Graham Barry. He and the vicar were seated opposite Rachel and Amy.

Rachel got straight to the point. "Tell me what you know about the body in the church crypt."

"I know nothing. I have no idea what you're talking about."

For a man who'd just received such news, he looked more shifty than shocked. He knew something all right, Rachel was sure of it. "You disappeared pretty sharpish when you knew we intended to search the crypt — coincidence, was it?"

"Look here, d'you imagine for one moment that I could have continued as normal knowing there was a body under my feet?" He gave Rachel a withering look. "You're deluded. You're keen to pin this on whoever you can find, and I just happen to fit the bill."

"You were quick to absent yourself once you knew about the search. That is suspicious in my eyes. Where were you going?"

"It's quite simple. I thought I'd get out of your way. Leave you to it. I did try to persuade George to come with me — have a spot of lunch, a walk in the hills — but he wasn't keen, so I went alone."

"Not good enough, Mr Neville. You're lying. It's written all over your face."

Neville lowered his head. "Have it your own way, but you're wrong. I am not the man you want. I do not kill people, Inspector. It goes against everything I believe in."

"Well, if the murders of that young girl and Mary Dunn were not down to you, I believe you know who did commit them." Rachel fell silent for a few seconds. "I want you to talk to me, tell me everything you know about what happened. If you are in danger, we will protect you."

Neville turned to his solicitor. "Please, will you tell them that I don't need protection. I can't help them because I know nothing. I'm the vicar of an inner-city parish, not a killer. I might have caught sight of the odd bit of dealing, but that's the extent of it."

"And you're sure you're not being blackmailed or coerced in any way to stay silent about what you know, Mr Neville?" Amy asked.

"Threatened, you mean? No, of course not," He shook his head. "It would be a useless exercise anyway. I am not easily scared."

"What about your brother?" Rachel asked. "What's he been up to?"

"Oh, so now you believe George has been rampaging round doing people in. You people are mad." Neville looked Rachel in the eye. "You've had it in for me since the first moment we met. I saw it in your face. But know this, Inspector, I have done nothing wrong and nor has George. My brother is an accounts manager for an insurance firm, not a murderer. You need to take that on board. Leave us alone and go and find the real perpetrators."

The solicitor cleared his throat. "D'you have any actual evidence to prove your accusations against my client?"

The short answer to that was no. Rachel was working entirely on her gut feelings and the fact that Neville had run when they were about to find the body. "Okay, you're free to go. But know this, Mr Neville, you remain a person of interest."

CHAPTER TWENTY-FIVE

Not the outcome with Neville that Rachel wanted but what else could she do but release him? He hadn't given anything away in the interview, and there was no forensic evidence to link him to either killing.

After a quick cup of coffee, Rachel and Elwyn set out for the morgue. "I still don't trust Neville," she said. "Even if the killings aren't down to him, I'm convinced he knows something. The man is a good actor and he sticks to his script."

"You could be right," he said. "It is his church, so you'd imagine he'd be aware of what was going on. But on the other hand, he might not. And if he did suspect someone or saw something, would he intervene? He'd know he'd be risking his life. If it was Arlo Bain who killed that girl, I imagine Neville would be terrified for his own safety. That young man is fast earning some reputation for himself."

"We find Arlo Bain and bring him in. Then we speak to Ronan Dunn. I'm sure the pair of them are mixed up in this somewhere," Rachel said.

"What about the drug squad?"

"Sod them, Elwyn. If the position was reversed, they wouldn't lift a finger to help us, so why should we hold back?"

They pulled into the car park. They had just started walking towards the hospital main entrance when a woman called out to Elwyn.

"Tina," he said to Rachel. "Give me a minute, I'll have a quick word then I'll join you."

Rachel gave the woman a friendly smile. She was a tad shorter than Elwyn, a slender attractive blonde, nothing like his ex-wife, Marie. He'd done well for himself.

* * *

Dr Butterworth was just beginning his examination of the body when Rachel joined him. "She was wearing a chain around her ankle. It's made of a thin metal, tarnished, and her legs were dirty, so it was easily missed by the killer. There's a small plate with something scratched on it, though I can't for the life of me make out what it says."

"Could be her name," Rachel said hopefully. "Will you let Forensics take a look, see if the lettering can be enhanced any?"

"She'd been dead for roughly a week when you found her. Decomposition hasn't got going yet so that's in our favour. Prior to ending up in that church, the poor girl had had a hard time of it. There are bruises, open wounds and scars on her body from beatings, and her left arm had been broken."

Rachel looked at the teenage girl laid out in front of her and a lump came to her throat. "How old was she?"

"Somewhere between sixteen and eighteen."

"How did she die?"

"I would say painfully," Butterworth said. "She was fastened by the wrist to that metal ring set into the stone wall. She suffered a series of beatings before being shot through the heart."

Rachel felt the tears well up in her eyes. Despite all her efforts to remain detached, this case was getting to her. It was the age of the victims — an elderly pensioner and a young teenage girl. "It sounds to me as if someone wanted something from her, information perhaps."

"Or perhaps she'd upset someone, Rachel. We retrieved the bullet, and it was fired from the gun you found, the one with 'Ghost' inscribed on it. Find the owner and you probably have your killer."

Rachel's instincts were on Arlo Bain owning that gun. She had no logical reason for thinking that other than her gut. Was that enough? "We've a few more tests to run on the body. The stomach contents will have to wait until we open her up but we can do bloods and a drugs screening. Plus, her clothing may give us something, though I doubt it was her own — everything was too big — and would have been expensive to buy new. From the state of her body, Jude and I both agree that she'd been on the streets for a while. It's possible she got the clothes from a hostel."

If he was right, Jonny might get something when he asked around later.

"That's about it for now," he said, covering the body.

"Get anything else, Colin, let me know."

On her way out, Rachel met Elwyn coming in to join her.

"Sorry for the delay. That was Tina by the way, sorry I didn't get to introduce you. She was in a bit of a state. She's being made redundant. Twenty years she's worked for that firm, and now a spat with the boss and she's out on her ear. The poor woman has no idea how she's going to manage. She has a mortgage, two teenage lads and bills to pay."

Rachel heaved a sigh. Tina had looked pleasant enough, but all her instincts were telling her that the woman was taking Elwyn for a ride. What was the betting he'd told her about his recent windfall? Was she looking to cash in? "Yes, that is a blow, but she's young and presumably has a good work record. She shouldn't find it too hard to find something else."

"That's exactly what I told her, but Tina isn't so sure. She's in house sales and apparently there's a slump."

Hmm. Rachel wasn't aware of that, and she'd had her eye on the housing market recently. It looked buoyant enough to her. "How did she know you'd be here?"

"I told her last night."

Rachel knew he wouldn't be pleased but this was Elwyn, and he'd do the same for her. "Please tell me she's not asked you for money," she said. "I know you of old and I know what a soft touch you are. Tina tells you a sob story, turns on the waterworks and you give her whatever she wants."

Elwyn frowned. "You're a hard woman, Rachel King. Tina isn't like that, and as for finding another job, she doesn't have your resilience."

Rachel bit her tongue. There was a lot more she could have said, pointed out that this job business was all a bit sudden, but she held back. Poor Elwyn. No sooner had he come into money than this new lady friend had come crawling out of the woodwork and suddenly become very needy. "Just be careful. I don't want to see you taken for a ride. I'm your friend, remember."

CHAPTER TWENTY-SIX

DC Jonny Farrell left early and went home to ditch the suit he wore for work and change into something more casual. He planned to visit the hostel on Oldham Road, speak to a few of the regulars, show them the photo, and if he got no joy, he'd have a wander round to Piccadilly Gardens and ask there.

Despite not being a particularly cold night, the hot soup served with a roll was as popular as ever. A crowd had gathered round a brazier. One of them, a tall man known on the streets as 'Marshy', beckoned Jonny over.

"It's our favourite copper," he said clapping the detective on the back. "What're you up to? Chasing the bad guys as usual?"

Jonny smiled and shook his head. This young man had helped him before. He was a useful pair of eyes and ears on the Manchester streets and didn't miss much. "No, Marshy. Actually, I'm looking for a girl." He took the photo from his jacket pocket and showed him. "She's met with a sticky end and I'm trying to find out who she was so I can tell her family — you know the sort of thing."

Marshy stared at the image for a moment or two. "Nice looking bird. Young though. If she ended up on the streets there's plenty who'd take advantage, use her to sell drugs if you get my drift."

"Anyone in particular taking on youngsters currently? Anyone new?"

Marshy shrugged. "Just the usual suspects. Some wealthy bloke, and there's a new firm making a name for themselves. They're operating around Ancoats."

Jonny reckoned Jacob Gilbert was the wealthy bloke and Arlo Bain was in Ancoats, though he had no way of proving that. "Names would be useful."

Marshy shook his head. "Don't have any, just the gossip."

"Would you be prepared to look at some mugshots at the station, see if anyone stands out?"

Marshy shook his head. "Daren't risk it, copper. I get found out and I'll end up in the canal. These people don't hesitate, as well you know. They'll put a bullet through your brain soon as look at you."

Jonny nodded. He understood. "Okay, Marshy, no sweat. I'll ask around and see what turns up."

"There's a bloke sleeps most nights in that shelter over in the gardens. He's called Robbie Stewart. There's not a lot happens without him knowing the ins and outs. Have a quiet word, say I sent you. He's fearless he is, has no problem dobbing in the bad guys."

Jonny said his goodbyes and started towards Market Street and Piccadilly. The place was busy. It was the rush hour and people were doing a bit of last-minute shopping before heading for home. Darkness was falling and there was a growing chill in the air. It was late September and the nights were drawing in. The poor sods stuck on the streets would soon be feeling the pinch.

On reaching the gardens, Jonny followed the path towards the shelter Marshy had mentioned. He could see someone on the bench, a man in his fifties.

"Robbie Stewart?"

"Who wants to know?"

Jonny sat down beside him. "I'm a friend of Marshy's. We've just had a word and he said you might be able to help me."

Robbie eyed him suspiciously, taking a swig from a whisky bottle. "What's it worth, this help you want?"

Jonny nodded at the bottle. "Enough to buy you another one of those."

That swung it. "Go on then, let's hear it."

Jonny passed him the photo. "Have you seen her?"

Robbie studied the image then passed it back quick. "She used to be one of Bain's. Ran drugs for him around the northern quarter and Ancoats for a while. She had a bit of trouble with you lot. I remember Bain complaining about it. Her and young Ronan got themselves busted. Bain doesn't like it when his people get themselves known by the police."

"When was this?"

"A couple of months ago. After that she just disappeared. I asked Bain about her, I liked seeing her around, pretty little thing she was. But he said she was looking for a way to get home, wherever that was."

"Name?"

"Now you're really asking." Robbie glanced at him. "Double the cash and I might remember something."

Jonny handed over two twenty-pound notes and waited.

"She got me some soup one night and we had a chat. She wasn't like the rest, didn't belong on the streets, that was obvious. I asked her name but she wouldn't tell me. Said it was safer all round if no one knew who she was. But she did say that she'd run away from home and had no intention of going back. Her father was some sort of brute who kept trafficked girls slaving for his wife at his home. This girl couldn't stand it anymore, saw a chance to get out and took it."

Gilbert, had to be, Jonny thought. "Did she say how she'd got out?"

"A lot of luck, that's all she said."

"Did she mention any other names?"

"Arlo Bain. She said he helped a few of the trafficked girls if they got free. I reckon Bain is after starting up on his own."

The information was useful — that's if it was true. First off, they needed to find Arlo Bain and bring him in for questioning. That young man was everywhere in this case. "Any idea where we can find Bain?"

"He'll likely be at that fancy flat of his in Ancoats. Bright House it's called — that is if he's still there. But even if he isn't, Gilbert's wife has a nephew living there. Worth a close look at I'd say. I'll lay odds that pair do business together. After all, his aunt is married to a Gilbert."

He meant Tara, the sister buried in the churchyard. "Thanks, Robbie, stay safe."

It'd been a good night's work. If what Robbie had told him was correct, there would be a record of the girl's arrest. First thing in the morning he'd check the system and see where they were up to with finding Bain.

CHAPTER TWENTY-SEVEN

The drive home took Rachel well over an hour. She arrived at the house exhausted, wanting nothing more than a hot bath and bed. However, as soon as she walked in through the front door she knew that something was wrong. The house had a strange vibe, it was oddly quiet. She tried to put it down to exhaustion but it was more than that. She called out but got no reply. A note left on one of the kitchen cabinets told her that Megan was with Jason again, and Mia was with Chloe, which left only Len.

"Sofia!" she called. There was no reply. Rachel went upstairs, presuming she'd got the lad in bed already and was resting herself. But Len's cot was empty and there was no sign of Sofia.

Rachel felt her stomach tighten with fear. Where were they? Had something happened to her son? Taking out her mobile, she rang Sofia, after a couple of tries there was no answer. Next she rang Mia.

"I'll have to be quick," Mia said urgently. "We're queuing in the pizza place in the village and we're just about to get served."

"D'you know where Sofia and Len have gone?"

"No idea. We all had something to eat about four and then I went round to Chloe's."

"Mia, this is important. Neither Sofia nor Len are in the house. Think carefully. Did Sofia say if she was going anywhere?"

"No, Len's been a grumpy little lump all afternoon and she couldn't wait to get him to bed."

"Not ill, just grumpy?"

"Yes, Mum. She's probably gone to see Belinda."

That was a possibility. "I'll ring her."

Rachel called her but had no joy. Belinda hadn't seen or heard from Sofia all day.

"I'm worried," Rachel said. "It's dark outside, so she can't have taken him for a walk. I'm at a loss, Belinda. If Sofia doesn't show within the next ten minutes, I'll have to ring the police."

"Rachel, you are the police," Belinda said gently. "Look, Alan and me will come round. Don't worry, there's probably a simple explanation."

"I can't just sit here and do nothing."

"Sofia could simply have nipped out to the shop. She'll be back any minute, you'll see."

But Rachel wasn't to be appeased. Deep inside she sensed that something had happened, something bad. The minutes ticked by and still there was no sign of them. Rachel paced the kitchen floor until, finally, she rang Elwyn. "Len is missing. I'm going out of my mind with worry. What have I done, Elwyn? I've been stupid. I took on a girl without bothering to check on her properly. I was short of time, far too gullible and desperate."

"Photograph her certificates and text them to me. I'll do a quick check now."

Sofia's portfolio was still on the coffee table where Rachel had left it. She took the photos and texted Elwyn. All she could do now was wait.

* * *

116

It took Elwyn only ten minutes to check Sofia's qualifications. What he discovered was terrifying. All of them were fake. Whatever experience Sofia had with children, hadn't been got at the college or nursery school she had named in her resume.

Amy was still at her desk, working. "We've got a missing toddler," he told her. "Len King, Rachel's little boy. It's looking highly likely that the au pair has kidnapped him."

Amy stared at him, gobsmacked. "Do I put out a call?"

"Yes. Local first and if we get no response we'll take it countrywide. This will be treated as urgent. Len is the son of a high-ranking CID officer and his disappearance is a serious matter."

Elwyn gathered together his notes and went to bring Superintendent Kenton up to speed.

"You're sure the girl hasn't just gone to see a friend?" Kenton said.

"I doubt it. She's new to the area and doesn't know anyone. Plus Rachel had insisted she keep to the infant's familiar routine."

Kenton still looked sceptical. "This young woman has only been looking after the kid two minutes. If she's new to the area, she could have gone out and got lost. We'll go with the local alert but keep me posted. Find him and call the troops off straight away."

"Rachel is worried, sir. She knows something is wrong."

Kenton didn't appear concerned. "And this girl didn't take the car?"

Elwyn shook his head.

"Okay, keep things local for the next couple of hours and if we get nowhere we'll do a media appeal. Meanwhile, get a team to do a sweep of the area around Rachel's house."

* * *

Rachel couldn't simply wait in the house for something to happen. Grabbing her mobile, she went out into the lane with the intention of speaking to the neighbours — not that she had many. There was really only the small farm across the road. The woman who owned it had been spending a lot of time at the front of her property recently, redoing the paintwork. She may have seen something.

And she had. "A van, love, about three this afternoon. The reason I noticed was because of the shouting. That young woman staying at yours didn't seem too thrilled at going with them."

"Going with who?"

"Two blokes, I think. I couldn't see clearly because of the hedge, but I heard their voices. One sounded older than the other."

"And you're sure Sofia and my Len were with them?"

"Yes, but under protest. She got into the front with the little one, and they put his pushchair into the back of the van."

"Did you see the number plate?"

The woman shook her head. "Sorry, love, I didn't realise it was important."

It was every bit as bad as she'd feared. On her way back to her own house, Rachel rang Elwyn and gave him the news. "Two men have been here and taken Sofia and Len. They were seen, so there is no doubt."

"I'm on my way, don't worry. We've mobilised the troops. We'll do everything we can to find them."

CHAPTER TWENTY-EIGHT

By the time Elwyn reached Rachel's house, she was going out of her mind with worry.

"I've heard nothing. If this is a kidnapping there's been no ransom demand. My neighbour from over the road saw Sofia and Len getting into a van. It seemed like Sofia didn't want to go. Unfortunately, my neighbour didn't think to get the number plate."

"He's a small child, he needs feeding, taking care of. We'll hear something soon," Elwyn said soothingly.

"Len has a strict routine. Deviate from it and he gets tetchy." Rachel dabbed at her tears. "He cries a lot, can be a right pain. I'm afraid that a couple of gangsters won't put up with his ways. Oh, Elwyn, they might just decide to silence him for good. And if they find out who he is, that he's Jed McAteer's son, God knows what they'll do."

"Don't, Rachel. You aren't doing yourself any good spouting rubbish like that. You've no idea what's happening. Your imagination is running away with you, and giving yourself all this grief for nothing does no one any good. And, anyway, he's got Sofia. She'll look after him."

"There's only so much she can do though," Rachel said. "She's a young woman, built like a beanpole. She's no match for a couple of blokes."

Belinda and Alan arrived and busied themselves in the kitchen making a pot of tea. "Elwyn's right," Belinda said when she brought it in. "Sofia might be a fraud but she does love kids. I spotted it straight away, that bit of her CV is genuine enough."

Rachel couldn't simply ignore what Elwyn had told her. The girl was a fraud and that made her a risk. Rachel had reached the point when she doubted she could take much more. She was quietly going out of her mind listening to all the theories, the possibilities about what might have happened to her son. She was about to burst into tears when her mobile rang. It was Mark Kenton.

"It looks like we've found him," he said. "I'm almost certain it's him, has to be. No one has claimed the child and he's causing a right ruck. He was found screaming his head off in the bakery aisle of a supermarket in Audenshaw. He's in the paediatric department at the hospital now."

"Is he . . . hurt?"

"No, he was taken there for a check-up just to be on the safe side. He's just tired and fed up, according to the doctor. Jude has asked if you can pick him up and bring a change of clothes. She'll run tests on the ones he's wearing, see if she can get anything on whoever took him."

Relief didn't cut it. Rachel had never been in so much terror and pain as she had in the last hour or so, and suddenly it was all gone. She looked at Elwyn, a silly grin on her face. "Good news. He's been found safe and well. Would you mind taking me to the hospital? I doubt if I could drive."

"Look, that's on Elwyn's way home, suppose I follow and bring you back," Belinda suggested. "We'll leave Alan here to look after the girls when they surface."

Rachel nodded. All she wanted now was to have her three children safely home. She turned to Alan. "Ring the girls, tell them what's happened and get them to come home. Tell Megan she can bring Jason with her if she must."

Rachel followed Elwyn out to his car. She was exhausted and at the end of her tether. "I've had it," she said climbing into the front passenger seat. "This is the last straw. I can't carry on like this. I live too far away from the station, and I haven't got anyone to look after the kids."

"Alan and Belinda appear to be doing a good job of it."

"The girls, yes, but Len isn't even Alan's. He's the child of his rival for goodness' sake. How d'you think that makes him feel?"

"He never lets it show."

"No, Elwyn, he never has, Alan is one of a kind. But it must hurt. Len is a constant reminder of everything that went wrong in our marriage. It was always Jed for me, and I just couldn't make it work with Alan."

* * *

As soon as she entered the ward, Rachel heard her youngest screaming his head off. She and Elwyn followed the noise and found Jude doing her best to quieten him down.

"I'm trying not to touch his clothing," she explained. "There's some sort of dust on his coat and I don't want to risk contaminating the samples we'll take."

The moment Len spotted his mum, his face broke into a grin. He stood up in the cot and held out his arms to her.

"Take off his clothes and then you can cuddle him," Jude said, smiling.

Elwyn handed her the clean set she'd brought. "His favourite pyjamas with the cars on them."

"We will be able to get CCTV from the supermarket," Jude said. "Apparently, a young woman brought him into the supermarket in his pushchair. She left him on the very aisle that has the camera. That could have been deliberate, so that he'd be found quickly."

"It sounds to me as if Sofia was trying to ensure that Len was safe."

While Rachel undressed the little lad, Jude held out an evidence bag for her to drop his clothing into. "I reckon so, and possibly putting herself in danger in the process, we just don't know."

The clothes he'd been wearing bagged up and Len dressed, Rachel picked him up and held him close. "I won't be in tomorrow, Elwyn," she said. "I can't, not when I've got a situation like this."

"It's Saturday tomorrow anyway. I'll carry on with the case and bring you up to speed on Sunday. I'll give you a ring before I drop in."

"You're entitled to a weekend too, Elwyn. What will Tina say?"

"I have warned her about the job, so I'm hoping she'll understand."

Rachel gave him a hug. He was a good man and she hoped that this Tina was not planning to trick him out of his inheritance.

CHAPTER TWENTY-NINE

Saturday

The following morning the team were gathered as usual. Elwyn began by apologising. "Sorry to drag you in at the weekend. You know I wouldn't if it wasn't necessary. And you'll note that we're missing our leader." He smiled, seeing Amy's face fall as she looked towards Rachel's desk.

"Rachel won't be back until Monday. We all have to realise that she's had a fright and a half, even you Amy. But we've been lucky and little Len is safe home with his mum. Jude is testing his clothing, and we've got CCTV from the supermarket where he was left."

"Are we working on the theory that Len's kidnap is connected with the case we're working on?" Amy asked. "Or is it . . ." She hesitated. "Well, we all know about the DCI's history with Jed McAteer."

Elwyn looked disapproving. "You're not even close. Jonny has discovered some interesting information. We're working on the theory that Rachel's au pair, Sofia, and the dead girl knew each other. Sofia was trafficked into this country by a gang run by Jacob Gilbert and set to work in his house. The same goes for the dead girl in the crypt."

"Does that mean we go after Gilbert?" Amy asked.

"I'll have to run that one past Rachel first. Gilbert has an army of legal people to call on, so we need to have a water-tight case before we tackle him. What we do first is get all the background we can on this gang and their activities. Jonny, you get on with that. We also need to ramp up the search for Arlo Bain. Amy, take a couple of uniformed officers and check that apartment of his in Ancoats. You can look at the one where Tara's son lives too, it's in the same block. If you get no luck there, ask around. Bain is well known, so some-one must have an idea where he is."

Jonny was fine with the task, but Amy was pissed off and said so. "I had a date later. So much for that."

"The sooner we get somewhere, the sooner we finish," Elwyn said.

Amy shot him a look and began shuffling through the paperwork on her desk.

"I'll get you the details — Bain and Shepherd's addresses and so on," he told her.

"D'you reckon the creepy vicar knew anything about the dead girl having worked for the Gilberts?" Jonny asked.

"That could be why he's been so reluctant to speak to us. Cross Gilbert and the outcome is dire. He's a man who doesn't give second chances. Neville could have been warned off, even paid to keep his mouth shut. That's something else we'll look into."

Elwyn went into Rachel's office and found the informa-tion Amy would need. "We'll meet back here at about two, see what we've got." Handing Amy the paperwork, he said to her, "Having Arlo Bain in custody would make my day. Rachel would be pretty chuffed too."

* * *

The apartment block was new and overlooked the marina. "Impressive," Amy said to the uniformed officer accompanying her. "There's certainly more money in dealing drugs than there is in police work."

He grinned at her. "You don't mean that. You'd never give up the job,"

"Oh, I might, Constable. The way things are going I doubt I can take much more. What with the hours, the workload and the high and mighty DCI King to cope with, it's all getting too much."

Constable Arran Copeland checked the address. "We need the top floor. Seems our Arlo has made the penthouse his home."

"Daniel Shepherd lives on the first floor, we'll check on him first," Amy decided.

They took the stairs, found his front door and pressed the bell. No response.

"Not in?" PC Copeland said.

"Or keeping out of our way. We'll catch him another time. Jonny's looked into that side of the family and not found much, so we'll concentrate on Bain for today."

They got the lift to the top of the building. The penthouse apartment was the only one on this floor and, listening at the door, the pair could hear sounds inside.

"Has he got someone with him?" Amy queried.

"I think it's the telly. Sounds like he's watching the football."

Amy rang the bell and waited. She didn't wait long. Seconds later, a tall young man with close-cropped dark hair opened the door.

She smiled at him. "Arlo Bain?"

"Who wants to know?"

Amy flashed her warrant card. "I'd like you to come down to the station for a chat."

"And if I refuse?"

"I wouldn't do that, mate," PC Copeland said behind her. "That would mean we'd have to create a scene and drag you out of here handcuffed, looking for all the world like a common criminal. Now, Mr Bain, I'm sure you don't want your smart neighbours to see that, do you?"

Bain gave the pair a filthy look. He tried to dodge past them, but Amy stuck her foot out. He fell flat on his face.

"Easier to simply come in for that chat, I'd say."

CHAPTER THIRTY

Having refused the services of a solicitor, Arlo Bain was with Amy in an interview room, PC Arran Copeland standing by the door. Bain was a big bloke and Amy was wary. But she'd asked specifically if she could do this alone. After a conversation about dos and don'ts, Elwyn had finally agreed.

"Where d'you work, Mr Bain?" she asked him.

"Oh, you know, here and there." He waved his arm casually. "Can't seem to settle to anything, you know how it is."

Amy wasn't impressed. "People don't get to live in fancy apartments like yours without a proper income. The rent alone must run to several hundred a month."

"I have contacts, friends who help me out." He grinned. "You really mustn't worry about me, I manage just fine."

"Is one of those friends Jacob Gilbert? You work for him, don't you?"

Arlo Bain stared at her for a moment then shook his head. "I've no idea who you're talking about. I've never heard of any Jacob Gilbert, love."

"You see, Mr Bain, I think you deal drugs for him and that's where you get the money to pay for your fancy apartment."

Bain heaved a sigh. "You know the mistake you're making, don't you? You're trying to rush me. Trying to make me confess to something I didn't do. If that's your game, you need more practice. For instance, you came straight out with it, you didn't hold anything back. Played all your cards at once, so to speak. You need to show a little more finesse, Detective Constable."

Finesse. How dare he? Amy wasn't having this. She wasn't going to sit there and let some no mark dealer tell her how to do her job. "You're in no position to criticise. Persist in withholding information and I'll lock you up. A night in the cells might loosen your tongue."

"No, love, a night in the cells will simply earn me a bit more street cred. Go ahead, do your worst. You can't keep me long anyway, you've no evidence."

"You have no idea what evidence we've got. For all you know we could have chapter and verse on you, and your operation."

"But I do know and what I know is you've got nowt. There's nowt to get."

Amy was sick of this. His cocky attitude was really pissing her off. "How can you be so sure?"

He leaned forward. He was laughing at her. For several seconds he stared at her, straight in the eyes. "Because I'm Job, love. I'm undercover drug squad."

Amy swallowed, her throat suddenly dry. Finally, she said, "I don't believe you. You're just saying that so you'll be released."

"You'll be releasing me anyway in a few minutes. Ring the drug squad and ask for Superintendent Swain, he'll tell you what's what."

With a nod to Copeland, indicating that he should to stay with him, Amy went into the main office to make the call. Was he telling the truth? Was he really working under-cover? If so, had she screwed up the job for him?

"Bain reckons he's undercover drug squad," she said to Elwyn. "I don't know whether to believe him or not. He's given me a number to ring. What d'you think?"

Elwyn disregarded the number on the scrap of paper and rang the offices of the squad direct. It wasn't a long conversation, and soon he'd learned as much as Swain was prepared to tell him. "Bain isn't lying. He's been undercover for several months. His brief is to get close to Gilbert so as to gather evidence against him. He's doing a good job too. That apartment he's living in is provided by Gilbert, as is the fancy car he drives. It's all geared to impress the punters. Swain wants us to back off immediately and leave him to get on with it."

"He can't help us then," Amy said.

"He knows a great deal about Gilbert's operation but will he tell us anything? Swain was adamant. We must put Bain back out there straight away. He reckons that by now Gilbert will know that Bain has been arrested, and should information get out that Gilbert would prefer to stay secret, he'll know who to blame." Elwyn considered the situation for a moment. "You stay here. I'll go and have a word myself."

"Got your answer then," Bain said. "You'll understand that I can say very little. Gilbert thinks I've been talking, he won't hesitate to kill me."

"I'm not interested in Gilbert's dealing for now. I just want to know about a young girl, early teens, who could have worked for the Gilberts."

"There was lots of young girls, they were Gilbert's thing. Used to drive Lauren mad." Bain grinned.

"Can you think of any who just disappeared out of the blue?" Elwyn asked.

Bain looked thoughtful. "There was one. I don't know her name or anything else about her. She worked in the house, running after Lauren mostly. She disappeared one night and I haven't seen or heard of her since. Could that be the one?"

Elwyn nodded. "Possibly. If it is, then she's turned up dead in a church crypt in Ancoats. Beaten, chained to the wall and finally shot."

"Gilbert," Bain said at once. "That's his style. If she ran and he caught up with her, that's what he'd do."

"D'you know her name, this trafficked girl?"

"No idea. Never took much interest."

"Okay, thanks. You might as well get off home."

"Tell that young female detective no hard feelings, will you? I wasn't taking the mick."

Elwyn smiled. "Our Amy doesn't hold grudges."

Elwyn returned to the incident room and added the new information about the dead girl to the whiteboard. He turned to the team. "Not a word about Bain beyond this room, understand. It gets out about who he really is, it could mean his life. We don't want that on our hands, do we?"

CHAPTER THIRTY-ONE

Monday

Work was the last thing Rachel needed right now, but what choice did she have? She had a murder case on her hands and to date, they had very little. One way or another she had to get it sorted so she'd have the time to make the much needed changes to her private life. This morning she'd had to leave little Len with Belinda again. She hated being reliant on her.

The team had been told to gather in the incident room early, so by eight they were all present. Jonny didn't look as if he minded too much but Amy was glaring daggers. There was obviously something on her mind and it seemed to be taking every ounce of her self-control to hold back.

"It's having to work over the weekend," Elwyn whispered in Rachel's ear. "These days work is coming a very poor second in Amy's world."

Rachel had no sympathy for her at all. Amy was a single woman with no responsibilities. She had a great job with good prospects and should be making the best of it.

"I want us to go over everything we've got," Rachel told them. "Every little detail, to ensure we've missed nothing important. Over the weekend Elwyn and Jonny put their new findings on the system so I'm up to date with Arlo Bain's position and that our dead girl possibly knew Sofia. But the latter is still very much in the realm of possibility, as yet we have no proof."

"I've been thinking about that," Elwyn said. "If the theory is correct, then Sofia must have targeted you as a potential employer. Do you have any idea why?"

He was right. It was something Rachel had already asked herself. She intended to speak to Belinda later and find out exactly how she had met Sofia. "The woman who introduced us is currently looking after Len. I'll get a statement from her after work."

"We have some results in from Jude," Jonny said. "Not that they make a riveting read."

The only forensic results that loomed large in Rachel's mind were the ones gleaned from Len's clothing. She was hoping they would give an indication of who had taken him. "Did she say anything about my son?"

"No, ma'am, sorry, nor anything about the chain around the dead girl's ankle. They're still working on both. They've processed the prints taken from Mary Dunn's flat and found nothing out of the ordinary. Her own, her daughter's, Jack Fairhurst's, plus other residents of the block."

Rachel nodded. It didn't help but it was no more than she'd expected. "I want a call putting out for Sofia Henshall, although the surname might not be correct. Both Elwyn and Jonny have information that suggest she is Eastern European, and I must say, she did have an interesting accent." She pinned a photo of Sofia to the board. "I have no idea where she is now, but make finding her a priority."

"Is she in trouble, ma'am?" Amy asked, stifling a yawn.

Rachel gave a sigh. Amy looked worn out. They'd all been working hard, and the sooner this was over the better.

"From what I've been told she wasn't instrumental in kidnapping Len. She was just as much a victim as he was. But we can't be sure of anything until we speak to her. Bear in mind also that Len was found, and I tend to believe that was down to Sofia, and I will be forever grateful for that. We should also speak to Henry Neville again and Daniel Shepherd. Elwyn and I will do that. I want to know if Shepherd is involved in this or not. He has the right family connections but until we know more we won't jump to conclusions." She turned to Amy. "When we first searched Mary's flat, we noticed that she had a collection of old newspapers. There are some in the hallway and others under the sink. Amy, go and collect them, take a look through and see if you can spot anything that might have upset Mary, something from the past that connects her to the Lawson or Gilbert families. Her friend Dotty told us that Mary had read something that bothered her. We should ask her if she can recall when this was."

She saw the look Amy threw her. She smiled encouragingly. "It could be important. And get PC Copeland to help you."

"Jonny, I want Jack Fairhurst's employment history going over. The dates he reckons he was in France and Spain are in the notes on the system."

She looked around at them all. "We'll meet after lunch, say, two this afternoon, and report back on what we've got. I want progress. Whoever killed Mary and that poor girl must be found and brought to book."

* * *

Jonny knew that checking Fairhurst's employment history would mean a visit to his flat to ask him for the exact dates he was abroad. Providing he was home and prepared to divulge the information, Jonny would then have to make a series of phone calls. But before he did any of that he'd check the system for the arrest of the girl Robbie Stewart had spoken about. Apparently, she was brought in at the same time as Bain, so hopefully this information should make his task easier.

And indeed it did. The date was recent, possibly within a day or so of her murder. Bain had been brought in for possession, kept overnight and then bailed the following morning. This had happened on a number of occasions, but this time he'd been accompanied by a young girl called Emma Smith. Was this her real name? Emma perhaps, but Jonny doubted the surname was correct. Anyway, they had her prints and DNA on file. Could she be the girl from the crypt? Working on a hunch that she was, he called Jude and gave her the details.

"After you've checked out our victim, would you look for any further DNA matches on the system, exact or familial, please?" he said.

"You have a theory?"

"I think a girl who was brought in with Bain a little while ago might be our victim from the crypt. But I'm also interested in finding out where she comes from, who her family are. It's just possible they have history with us too."

"Good call, Detective. I should be able to do that. I'll have an answer for you by tomorrow morning."

Jonny hoped this might be a quicker way of getting the girl's name than trawling through missing persons. That could take days. Days they didn't have.

CHAPTER THIRTY-TWO

Rachel and Elwyn parked up outside the church and went inside. Henry Neville was standing by the altar, his hands clasped in prayer.

"Reverend Neville," Rachel said. "We'd like another chat, if you don't mind."

"Not the police station again," he complained. "My parishioners will get the wrong idea and start to doubt me."

"Surely not. You're their vicar. How could they fail to support you in your hour of need?" Rachel nodded at a pew. "Sit down, answer our questions and we won't keep you long."

"I know nothing that will help you. You are talking to the wrong person."

"If that is the case, who is the right person?" Elwyn asked. "You know everyone who lives around here."

"I don't know what else I can tell you. I had no idea that poor girl was down there."

"The problem we have, Reverend, is that we don't believe you," Rachel said. "My people moved all the books off that shelving. It was heavy work, and shifting the bookcase itself needed several strong men. It took time, it was noisy and though they tried hard not to leave a mess, there was a lot of dust." Rachel looked around. "Which is still there."

Neville shook his head. "The killers must have done it at night. Or when I wasn't here."

"Have you been away for any length of time recently?" Elwyn asked.

"I paid a quick visit to my sister's last week," he told them. "That must have been when they . . . well. Did what they did."

"Murdered a young girl. Shot her in cold blood. That's what they did, Reverend," Rachel said.

Rachel saw the look of horror on his face. "You don't really think we believe the tale about your sister, do you? But if you insist on your story, we will check it out. Why not just talk to us? It might be easier."

"All right, all right, it was a lie. I haven't been anywhere."

"Just tell us what happened," Elwyn urged.

Neville glanced fearfully around the church, as if to make sure there was no one lurking about who might overhear. "I had no choice. I really didn't. But I swear I had no idea what they'd put down there. I never venture down those steps, and anyway, I was told to stay well away."

"Who're you talking about?" Elwyn asked. "Who told you?"

"I've no idea who they were. One of them was younger than the other. He was the one who threatened me. He had a gun and waved it in front of my face. Said I'd end up down there too if I didn't do as he said."

"When they said that, you must have realised they intended to kill the girl," Rachel said.

"I chose not to think about it. I know it was selfish and cowardly, and I'm not proud of it."

"Two of them, you said?" Rachel queried.

"Yes, two men, and they could obviously handle themselves. If I hadn't got out of the way, let them get on with it, they would have killed me too. Either way, the girl stood no chance."

Rachel shook her head, almost too angry to speak. "So, you just left them to it. You must have had an opportunity to ring the police, tell us what was happening. We would have been here within minutes, and perhaps the girl could have been saved."

"I was terrified. These two weren't simply dealers fooling around. They would have shot me too. Besides, they took my phone and locked me in the side room back there."

Was he telling the truth this time? Rachel still wasn't sure. Her gut told her there was still plenty that Neville wasn't saying. "Did the girl have a name?"

Neville shook his head. "I didn't recognise her. I don't think she was from Ancoats. When they dragged her in here, she was only semi-conscious. I doubt she was even aware of where she was. Neither of the men referred to her by name."

"And the two men, did they use names?"

Neville averted his eyes. "That's what made it worse. One of them called the other 'Ghost'. I've heard that name before, and he is not someone you mess with."

That was the name Hedley Sharpe had mentioned, and it was also engraved on the gun that shot the girl and killed her. Ghost had to be the one who was currently challenging Gilbert's position in the city. "When have you heard that name? In what context?"

"I chased some kids out of the graveyard one night and they threatened me with Ghost. Said they'd get him to come and sort me out."

"You're sure they were using the word as a name and not trying to frighten you?" Elwyn asked. "You were in a graveyard, after all. What made you so sure they weren't referring to the spirits of the dead?"

"I keep my ears open. I might wear this dog collar but I do know what's going on. Jacob Gilbert has a rival and he needs to be careful. This man Ghost is after what he has, and rumour has it that it's only a matter of time before he gets it."

Rachel was surprised at how much Neville knew. She'd leave his knowledge of the underworld for another time. She still didn't trust him. "I want you down at the station to make a statement. I'll be sending a car for you so don't go anywhere."

"I'm sorry if I've misled you, Inspector. That was never my intention."

"Misled? No, Mr Neville, it's more than that. You've withheld information that would have helped us. You should have told us everything at the start."

"You have to understand my position," he whined.

Ignoring his plea, she and Elwyn went back to the car, Rachel deep in thought. "Why here, Elwyn? Why bring a girl here and kill her?"

"Perhaps they've been to the church before, spoken to folk and know about the crypt. It's a perfect place to hide a body."

"It must be someone local in that case, someone who is familiar with the layout of the church. They could attend the services here, or are close to someone who does. And they not only know the church, I reckon they've got the measure of Neville too."

CHAPTER THIRTY-THREE

Rachel pressed the doorbell of Shepherd's flat and waited. Was it coincidence that Daniel Shepherd lived in the same apartment block as Arlo Bain? Or did Shepherd dabble in the drug trade too, and Bain was here to watch him? Bain hadn't mentioned him, so she thought she'd give Shepherd the benefit of the doubt.

A young man opened the door and smiled at them.

"Have you got time for a word?" Elwyn asked, showing him his badge.

The smile vanished. "What about?"

This was tricky. As far as they knew, Daniel Shepherd wasn't guilty of anything. He didn't really have anything to do with what they were investigating either. "When did you last see your aunt, Lauren Gilbert?" Rachel asked.

He rolled his eyes. "Always the same bloody question. You lot just won't leave me alone. Regular as clockwork, you come banging on my door asking about the Gilberts."

"It's a simple enough question, and could prove important to a case we're working on," Rachel said.

"For the last time, I have nothing to do with her or her old man. I haven't even seen them since my mother's funeral. The man's a villain and she's no better. I detest the pair of them."

Harsh words. Should they believe him? "This is a fancy apartment for someone who doesn't appear to have a regular income. I couldn't find any work record for you, Mr Shepherd. Can I ask how you afford it?"

"None of your business," he retorted. "But if you really want to know, I paid for it out of the money my mother left me in her will. It's no secret, feel free to check it out."

Shepherd was angry and rightly so. They'd descended on him out of the blue for no reason, and were asking him personal questions. What he'd told them was perfectly plausible, and as he said, easily checked.

"Look, I'm sorry, Mr Shepherd. We have no wish to upset you," Rachel said. "All we're trying to do is get a handle on a tricky murder case. We're speaking to everyone within the Gilberts' spere of influence."

"Well, he has no influence over me." Shepherd shook his head. "Sorry. I'm over-sensitive about where I come from, but who can blame me? Can you imagine what it's like having that pair as your closest relatives? Even Jacob's daughter has run away."

Rachel's curiosity was sparked. "They have a child? I didn't know that."

"Emma is Jacob's, not Lauren's. She's the product of an affair he had with a woman called Karen Darwin."

"How old is Emma?" Elwyn asked.

"Must be about sixteen, although I've not seen her since my mother's funeral."

"Any idea where we can find this Karen Darwin? Emma might be with her and we'd like a word."

"She lives somewhere out Oldham way, I believe. Look her up, you've got the resources — she's a registered heroin user."

"Thanks. We'll leave you in peace now." Rachel smiled at him. "Hopefully, we won't have to trouble you again."

Shepherd's information was useful. If they hadn't gone to see him, they wouldn't have known about Emma Gilbert. As they made for the car, Rachel wondered if Emma could be the girl in the crypt. "It's possible, isn't it? And given her mother is a user, we might have her DNA on record."

"I'll get Jude to check for familial DNA," Elwyn said as they pulled onto the main road.

"How did you know that's exactly what I was thinking?"

"Because I know you, Rachel King. Emma Gilbert is the same age as our victim. This character Ghost has a beef with Gilbert, the girl is taken, perhaps as a warning. It's straightforward enough."

"Let's hope you're wrong. But if his daughter is missing, why didn't Gilbert come to us? We might have been able to help."

"What? Gilbert? Given who he is, I doubt going to the police even crossed his mind. We'll ask Jude to look for a DNA match with Gilbert too. He's had his prints and DNA taken often enough."

"Even so, we'll have to ask him, at least get a photo of his daughter to rule her out."

"Don't forget what Kenton said — no contact with Gilbert until you run it past him first."

While Elwyn drove, Rachel rang Jude and asked her to do the tests.

"Jonny has asked me much the same thing," Jude said.

Rachel smiled. "Clever lad, our Jonny. By all means do that, but look at Jacob Gilbert and one Karen Darwin first."

"Gilbert? I had no idea the man had a daughter," Jude said.

"Neither did we, and we have a horrible feeling that she might be our dead girl."

They were almost back at the station when Rachel got a call from Amy. She had some good news at last. "The girl Sofia has been brought in, ma'am. She was found hitching at a motorway service station on the M6."

Rachel heaved a sigh. Just the person she wanted to speak to. With any luck, Sofia would be able to add another piece to this puzzle.

"I'll interview Sofia and then we'll assemble the team for that feedback meeting," Rachel decided. "We could do with finding out for sure if Gilbert's daughter is missing and if he has a problem with this so-called rival, Ghost. Hedley Sharpe said as much, and now Neville. Sooner or later, we're going to have to have a conversation with Gilbert, and I for one am not looking forward to it."

CHAPTER THIRTY-FOUR

Sofia was seated in one of the interview rooms under the watchful eye of Arran Copeland. As Rachel entered the room, she gave her an apologetic smile.

"I had no wish for that to happen to your son, Mrs King. But I had no choice. If I'd refused to do as those men asked, the outcome would not have been good."

If the men she was talking about were Mary and the girl's killers, Rachel didn't doubt it. "One way or another your actions saved my son, and I am eternally grateful for that," Rachel said simply. "But I must say, the people we're after don't strike me as having much compassion."

"They couldn't cope with the noise. Len was crying — screaming at one point. He was hungry and cold. I told them it would be better to leave him somewhere he could be found. We struck a bargain. I'd tell them what they wanted and they would let him go."

"And what did they want, Sofia?"

"Information about the case you're investigating. They wanted to know if you'd identified the body of the girl found in the church."

"We haven't yet. What did you tell them?"

"Just that. I'm sorry but I photographed your notes. You leave your notebook in your jacket pocket most nights and I took it out while you slept."

Now for the big question. "Who wanted this information, Sofia?"

Tears rose in her eyes. She hung her head. "I tell you that and I am dead for sure. The man in charge of this operation is the very devil, and even you won't be able to protect me from him."

"Jacob Gilbert?" Rachel asked.

Sofia gave a small smile. "True, he is a bad man. Even though he's getting old and looking for a quieter life, he is vicious and vengeful." She pushed her hair back off her face, showing Rachel the bruising around her temple and eyebrow. "The two men who took me and Len were violent thugs but I don't think they worked for Gilbert. I was in the back of the van trying to quieten Len, and I could hear them whispering in the front. They spoke as if they were afraid of Gilbert, not working for him."

"How much d'you know about Gilbert?"

"I know he's a big-time drug dealer and people trafficker with a formidable reputation and that he's quick to kill those who cross him. I was brought into this country by his gang. It was a dreadful time. Dozens of us packed together in a small boat and made to cross the English Channel at night. When we arrived, we were herded into a truck like cattle. We didn't stop until Manchester. A lot of us got sick, they were older than me and it was cold. When we got there, we were taken to a huge warehouse. Gilbert was there and he was separating us into groups. He liked the look of me and said I'd be set to work in his home. I thought I'd landed on my feet, but I was nothing but a skivvy. At least I was in no danger. The only problem I had was Lauren, his wife. She was a jealous cow and picked on me all the time. There is no kindness in her at all. She treated me like a slave and she was no better with Emma, Gilbert's daughter. Emma complained to her father often enough but nothing changed. He simply told her to fight back."

"Okay, if it wasn't the Gilberts who took you, who did?"

"I didn't see their faces and I didn't get their names. The only one I did hear was 'Ghost'. I'd heard that name before, and I know him to be evil to the core."

Ghost again. He was everywhere, so why couldn't they discover his true identity? "What's he like? Young? Old?"

"Difficult to say with just a voice to go on. But it was gravelly, like he smoked. He was tall and he spoke like everyone else round here."

"Local then. And his friend?"

"He was bit younger I'd say. He never said a word, I just heard them whispering, so I couldn't tell what he sounded like."

"Did you see their faces?"

"No, they always wore those things over their head and faces — balaclavas, is it? But the younger one had light-coloured hair, not dark like mine."

"Are you prepared to testify against them and the Gilberts, Sofia?"

"Give evidence in court?" She looked horrified. "No. They'd kill me for sure. Jacob Gilbert is not a forgiving man. I still have family alive back home and he'd set his traffickers against them as well. They'd all be killed for sure."

"Did he get you to deal drugs too?" Rachel asked.

She hung her head. "He tried but I wasn't any good at it. I lost some heroin once because I was so nervous. That cost him a lot of money, so he didn't involve me again."

"You testify and we will make a good case against him. Then he will go to prison."

"I can't. Even then we wouldn't be safe. My family would still suffer, and, anyway, Gilbert has an army of lawyers. You would never win the case."

Rachel would have to broach the subject some other time. She had other things to think about for now. "Thank you, Sofia. A colleague of mine is going to join you shortly and he'll get you to write all that down." She gave Sofia a long, hard look. "You have told me everything, haven't you?"

The girl nodded.

"Was it you who told them where I lived?"

"No. When they took us that evening, they simply turned up on the doorstep."

Another pair of gangsters who knew where to find her. It meant that while the case was still active, she and her three children were in danger.

"What will you do now?" Rachel asked.

"I have some money saved, so eventually I intend to return home."

"One more question, Sofia. When you left the Gilbert's house, you took something from the safe."

"Drugs," Sofia said simply.

"And you sold them on?"

"Yes, to a young thug called Arlo Bain. I'd seen him with Jacob and knew he'd give me a fair price."

That sorted that one. And given Bain was drug squad if he'd been given the drugs, he'd hand them in which meant they would not hit the streets.

"What else did you take?" Rachel asked.

"There was a lot of jewellery. I could have helped myself, but I didn't." She hung her head. "Well . . . one piece did appeal to me. A small gold crucifix with diamonds on it."

Rachel nodded. That wasn't what she was interested in. "But you did take something else as well, didn't you? Think hard, Sofia. It might seem insignificant to you."

"It was just a black velvet bag with a lock of hair in it. I'm not sure what became of it. I didn't intend to take it but it was in the bag with the drugs and the crucifix, so I guess Arlo must have it."

That sorted the puzzle of the hair. But what had Arlo done with it? He had to have passed it on for it to end up on Mary Dunn's coat. Perhaps someone else had found it?

"Thanks, Sofia. One last thing, you must have known Emma Gilbert well. If I show you a photo, will you tell me if it's her?"

The only image they had was of the girl's body but her face was relatively unmarked. "You see, we've found a body and it may be Emma, but without help we can't identify her."

Sofia gave a little shudder but nodded.

"Thank you. I'll go and get the photo."

Rachel gestured for the officer to keep watch while she nipped out. She grabbed the photo and hurried back.

Sofia stared at the photo, blinking back tears. "They killed her, didn't they? Poor Emma. She didn't deserve that. She was a brave girl. Her father always told her to stand up for herself and she tried hard, particularly where Lauren was concerned. She was kind to me, too, and I will always be grateful to her for that."

"So that is definitely Emma Gilbert?" Rachel asked.

"Yes."

"Thank you. You are not in any trouble. As soon as you've given your statement you will be free to go."

Sofia looked at Rachel. "I will go home to my family soon, but in the meantime, I'd like to continue working for you. The children like me and I'm fond of them already."

Rachel didn't know what to think about that one. Dare she take the risk? Not if Sofia looked after them at home but there was an alternative. "That's a good idea but you can't simply go back to my house, not now those thugs know where I live. Let me speak to Belinda first, see if she can help."

"You are right to be careful, Mrs King. Those men could well come back, and this time things might not end so well. But I assure you I am being straight with you. I was forced at gunpoint to go with those men."

Rachel didn't doubt Sofia was telling the truth. "Give me a few minutes to make a call."

Given the killers were still out there, Rachel was well aware of what could happen, but she refused to disappear again. Her need for shorter hours and childcare was one thing, but no way was she turning tail and running away this time. Whatever was coming, she'd first ensure the kids were safe, and then face it head on. Between them, Belinda and Sofia could help her with that.

CHAPTER THIRTY-FIVE

Rachel went back to her office, rang Belinda and told her about Sofia.

"The girl's got some cheek wanting to pick up where she left off," Belinda said.

"She had no choice. She did her best given her situation, and remember, she did save Len from getting hurt. No, I think she's genuine. The problem I have is that we can't all go back to my house. Those killers know where I live and could easily come again."

"You want me and Alan to take the girls?"

"Yes, please, and Len too, if you wouldn't mind. I was thinking that Sofia could help you. Primarily with Len but she's good with Mia too. And it won't be for long, possibly a matter of days, just until we get this case solved."

Rachel crossed her fingers. It was a big ask.

"Okay," Belinda said finally. "I'll round them up this afternoon. I'll pick Mia up from school, text Megan, and Len's already here."

Rachel heaved a sigh of relief. This would take a weight off her shoulders. She'd be forever grateful.

"Do I have to take Sofia too?" Belinda asked.

Rachel knew that even with Sofia's help, Belinda would have her work cut out. "She is desperate to put things right. I've spoken to her and I believe what she told me."

"As long as you're sure."

"Thanks, Belinda. I'll put Sofia in a taxi. She should be with you in less than an hour."

"And what are your plans?"

"I intend to stay at home."

There was a pause. "Is that wise, given the situation?"

"I'm not running, not again," Rachel said.

"Stubborn to the end. Okay, but make sure you look after yourself and don't take any risks. Don't worry about the kids either, me and Alan will make sure they are all safe."

"One thing before I leave you to it, can you recall how you first met Sofia?"

"In Stockport library. She was looking for a job and using one of the computers. She was having a problem with the internet and was about to give up and leave when I helped her out. We got talking, went for a coffee and I took to her. There was nothing sinister in it."

"Okay. I'd better get back to the team. I'll ring you later."

* * *

With her business head on, Rachel went into the main office and stood in front of the whiteboard. "Right, team, what've we got?"

"I've got black newsprint dancing in front of my eyes," Amy complained. "I've gone through a huge pile of papers but I can't find anything that could have upset Mary Dunn."

"Jonny?"

"Fairhurst's work history checks out in both France and Spain. I also checked the records to see when Emma Gilbert could have been brought in. If we're looking at the right girl, she called herself 'Emma Smith' and was brought in with Arlo Bain, like he said."

"I believe she is the right girl," Rachel told them. "Sofia worked for the Gilberts and she's identified a photo of our victim as Emma." So far so good, but they still had no suspect. "Elwyn and I have discovered that Emma Gilbert's mother is one Karen Darwin, who lives in Oldham. Amy, I want an address for her. We will have to ask her when she last saw her daughter. The DNA tests Jude is currently running on the body from the crypt will prove her identity conclusively, but I want to rule out the possibility that we're chasing our tails here, and that Emma has simply run away and is staying with her mother."

Rachel looked at Jonny. "Anything come in from Forensics, by the way?"

"Only a message. Jude wants you to ring her."

Rachel nodded. That was next on her list. She started towards her office but stopped and spoke to Elwyn first. "Find out where Bain is today. I could do with a word. Sofia gave him the drugs she stole from the Gilbert house, and the lock of hair was with them. I want to know what became of it."

Elwyn followed in her wake, closing her office door behind him. "The kids sorted?"

"Yes. Belinda and Alan have stepped into the breach."

"What about keeping you safe?"

"I'll arrange something. I'll ask Kenton to get a couple of uniformed officers to stand guard. I'll also ask Jude if she can give me a tracking device. That way, you lot will always know where I am."

"You're determined to go home then. I was going to offer you a room at mine."

"Thanks, but there's no need. I won't run, Elwyn, not again."

Rachel reached into her drawer and took a couple of notes from the cash she kept in a box. "Will you ring for a taxi to take Sofia to Bollington as soon as, please? I'll just give her this for the fare."

It was kind of Elwyn to offer but she didn't want his mollycoddling this time.

CHAPTER THIRTY-SIX

With Sofia sorted and on her way to Belinda's, Rachel returned to the incident room.

"Jude's been on with some new information," Jonny said. "The cigarette ends and one of the beer cans found in the crypt have Jack Fairhurst's DNA on them."

Rachel groaned — this was all she needed. "I had hoped that no one connected with Kimberley Dunn was involved. That woman has had enough aggro recently to last her a lifetime."

"Well, like it or not, he was in that crypt, and Jude pointed out that the cigarette ends were close to the victim. She also said that during his preliminary examination of the body, Dr Butterworth has found evidence of small, round burns on her torso."

Cigarette burns. Rachel shuddered.

"Now I come to think of it, there was something in those newspapers," Amy said. "I dismissed it because I thought we'd decided Fairhurst was innocent."

"He was in the paper?" Rachel asked.

"Yes. It was an article about him finding some old piece of pottery on a beach in France. The French press made a lot more of it but he did get a mention in the local rag."

"Mary must have read it and realised he'd be coming home. Maybe that's why she was upset. Amy, go and have another word with Dotty. Ask her if Mary knew Fairhurst before Kimberley got involved with him."

Amy nodded. Finally, there was a smile on her face.

"Jude wants you to ring her about the post-mortem. Dr Butterworth is concerned that no one has come forward to identify the body, with her being so young," Jonny said.

"The DNA tests — nothing through on them yet?" Rachel asked.

"They will take another day at least."

"One witness has already identified the girl as Emma Gilbert," Rachel said. "But she isn't family, simply a friend and, as we know, Emma does have parents, although I really don't want to ask Jacob Gilbert to identify her. Once he knows his daughter has been brutally murdered, he could kick off a war out on the streets."

Elwyn cleared his throat. Swinging round, she saw that Kenton had entered the room.

"I'm concerned about the lack of progress in this case," he said bluntly.

"We are too, sir," Rachel said. "But we are making some progress. We have narrowed down our list of suspects and we'll interview them again."

He didn't look convinced. "Anything I can help with?"

He'd offered, so why not? "Dr Butterworth wants our youngest victim identifying by a relative before he's happy to do the PM. She's Jacob Gilbert's daughter. Unfortunately, that means we'll have to contact him."

"Unfortunate indeed. Leave it with me. I'll make the phone call myself and get back to you."

Then he was gone.

As the door closed behind him, Rachel heaved a sigh of relief. "Not a job I was relishing. I wonder if Gilbert will agree to come in."

"It's his daughter, so he's bound to," Elwyn said.

Rachel walked over to the whiteboard. While they had Gilbert under their roof, what else could they face him with? There were lots of possibilities but the problem was making anything stick.

Elwyn guessed what was on her mind. "This girl, Sofia. Is she willing to give a statement in court about Gilbert's trafficking?"

Rachel shook her head. "She's afraid that if she does, Gilbert will harm her family back home." She turned to face him. "That man has his operation well and truly stitched up. His operatives are terrified to put a foot wrong."

The door opened and Kenton walked back in. "I've just had an interesting conversation with Lauren Gilbert," he told the team. "She told me that Jacob is away and can't be reached. Beyond that, she wouldn't say, she wouldn't even tell me when he was due to return. As to identifying the body herself, she flatly refused."

They were back to square one in that case, and reliant on the DNA results. "We had to try," she said to Kenton. "But it does give us a problem, unless Butterworth is willing to continue regardless."

Jonny put down his phone with a smile on his face. "I might be able to help with that one. Karen Darwin is back at her old address in Oldham after a spell in rehab. Prior to that, she spent several weeks in hospital and had no visitors. It doesn't look like Emma went running to her. I've spoken to her and if there is a problem with her daughter then she wants to help."

Rachel wasn't surprised. There had been an outside chance that she had gone to her mother, but the more evidence they gathered — the clothes she was wearing for one — the more certain she was that the girl had managed to survive on the streets before falling foul of whoever killed her.

"I'll contact her," Rachel told Kenton. "She's the girl's mother and needs to be told anyway."

"Keep me informed," Kenton said, and left them to it.

"Thanks, everyone," Rachel said when he'd gone. "I'll give Jude a ring, give her the news. Jonny, find Amy and you and her bring Fairhurst in. And do it with the minimum of fuss. If possible, try not to upset Kimberley."

"What about Karen Darwin?" Elwyn asked.

"We'll have to bring her in. Give me a minute to speak to Jude and I'll be right with you."

Rachel went into her office and sat at her desk. She dialled Jude's number, while debating how best to tell a vulnerable woman that her child had been murdered.

"The post-mortem for the girl in the crypt," she began. "A friend of hers has identified her as Emma Gilbert from a photo."

"Colin's been fussing again. He's concerned that she's so young. She's a Gilbert, so she has parents. Colin's worried that if he does the PM without a parent having identified her, he'll anger Jacob. Get one of them to come in and identify her properly. Then we can get on with it."

"Her father is away," Rachel said. "He's not a nice man, thinks with his fists. I storm in and tell him his daughter's been brutally murdered and he could flip. But we do have contact details for her mother. She lives in Oldham, not too far away, so Elwyn and me are going to collect her. With a bit of luck, we should be with you in a couple of hours. Think Colin can delay until then?"

"No problem. Get her mother to the mortuary and he'll be able to tick all the boxes."

"Anything from Len's clothing?"

"No, the white powder on his coat turned out to be nothing more harmful than flour." She laughed. "The lad must have got a bit frustrated and pulled stuff off the shelves."

Rachel smiled. Just like him. "Thanks, Jude, see you later."

Back in the incident room, Rachel told Arran Copeland and his partner to find Arlo Bain and bring him in.

"A drugs matter, ma'am?" Copeland asked.

Rachel nodded. She wasn't going to say anything about the drug squad. "Put him in an incident room and watch him until I get back. Elwyn and I are off to Oldham and then the mortuary."

Rachel noticed Elwyn's shudder. She knew exactly how he felt. There were times when this job was the pits. On days like this she'd happily ditch it for a few shifts in Belinda's shop. It wasn't the occasional day either. In her heart of hearts she knew that enough was enough. It was time to find out exactly how much the house was worth and find a smaller place, realise some cash and get herself a far less demanding job.

CHAPTER THIRTY-SEVEN

The traffic was kind so it took them only twenty minutes to drive up the A62 to Werneth, the suburb of Oldham where Karen Darwin lived.

"Built-up and noisy," Elwyn noted as he locked the car, the heavy traffic whizzing by.

"No more so than Levenshulme," Rachel pointed out. "And it's convenient. Only a quick hop into the city."

"That what you're looking for? Somewhere closer to the station?"

What to tell him? Not the truth. He'd be mortified to know she was thinking of ditching the job altogether. "It's an idea, it would certainly make things simpler."

"Your daughters would complain. Your Mia's whole life is in that village where you live. Her mates, her school and she's at that age when fitting in somewhere else starts to get tricky."

"Now you're an expert on teenagers, I see," Rachel scoffed. "Believe me, Elwyn, you have no idea. But know this, I decide to make changes and the girls will have to fit in."

Rachel strode ahead and rang Karin Darwin's doorbell. The woman who answered eyed the pair suspiciously. "You police? Only Kaz got a call and she's been worried sick ever since."

"She isn't in any trouble," Rachel said, "but we do need a word."

The woman stood aside for the pair and pointed down the hallway. "Room at the end. Don't get her wound up 'cause it'll be me who has to deal with the fallout."

"You're her friend?" Elwyn asked.

"Yes, I'm the bloody fool who picks up the pieces and sticks 'em back together. Trouble is, Kaz is never quite the same afterwards."

The pair entered the sitting room to find a woman nervously pacing the floor. She was haggard-looking and much too thin.

"This is about our Emma, isn't it?" she said. "She's got herself into trouble, and I bet that bastard of a father of hers can't be bothered to help her out."

"It's not quite like that, Karen," Rachel told her. "The truth is, we've found a body and we think it might be your daughter, Emma."

Karen Darwin stared at her. "My Em? Dead? No, she can't be. I'm not much of a mother but I would have known."

Rachel took a photo of the girl from her pocket and showed it to her. "Is this her, Karen?"

Karen began to wail. "What happened? How come she's ended up dead?"

"We're still investigating," Elwyn said. "But it would help if you would come with us and identify her body."

Karen shook her head. "I don't know if I can, you know, see her like that. She was my daughter, don't you understand?"

Rachel cleared her throat. She understood well enough, but they were running short of time. "We want to catch whoever killed her, and I'm sure you do too."

"It's plain enough. Her father, that monster Jacob Gilbert, he killed her. It was always going to happen. Once she went to live with him there was no stopping it."

"We don't suspect him," Elwyn told her.

"No, but he has enough enemies. They wouldn't hesitate if they got their hands on Emma. She was always his weakness. I tried to tell him but he wouldn't listen, and neither would she."

"We believe Emma ran away, and that something happened the night she left that meant she never went back."

Karen sniffed. "That'd be down to Lauren. She was always jealous of Emma, hated the way Jacob doted on her. He could never decide which of them to side with. Lauren is forceful, she bullied Em. I knew she'd run away sooner or later."

"Didn't she contact you?" Rachel asked.

Karen looked away. "You have to understand, I've never been much cop on the parenting front. What with my habit and being constantly in and out of rehab, we stood no chance. If only she'd rung me, let me know she'd left Jacob. We could have worked something out."

Rachel checked the time. "We'd better get going."

"Jacob not got the balls, has he?" Karen said.

"We haven't been able to speak to him. We've been led to believe he's away. Lauren has been told, so I expect she'll let him know."

Karen shrugged into her coat. "I wouldn't count on it, love. That woman doesn't brook any interference in her marriage, and I'm afraid that's what she saw my Em as."

CHAPTER THIRTY-EIGHT

The pathologist, Colin Butterworth, was waiting for them at the mortuary. "Sorry to meet you under these circumstances," he told Karen gently. "I'm told the girl might be your daughter."

"I've seen the photo. It's my Emma all right."

Butterworth led the way to the viewing room. "You can look at her from behind the glass if it's easier for you," he said.

Karen shook her head. "I'd rather go in there if you don't mind. See her properly."

"Okay, but please don't touch her. Simply look at her face and tell me if it's your daughter or not. You can just nod."

Rachel and Elwyn hung back as Butterworth led Karen inside. He removed the sheet covering her face and stood back.

After several seconds, Karen nodded. "Yes, that's my Emma," she sobbed through her tears. "Did they hurt her? I couldn't bear it if she suffered."

Butterworth said nothing for a few moments and then shook his head. "I'll know more after the PM and when the forensic team have done their work," he said evasively.

"What happens now?"

"That's your job done." He smiled. "I'm sure DCI King will make sure you get home safely."

"I'll get a PC to drive you," Rachel said. "Thank you, Karen. Your identification has made it easier for us to find out what happened to your girl."

"You will let me know when I can make arrangements, won't you?" Karen asked. "I want to bury her properly."

Rachel nodded. "Don't worry, we'll be in touch in plenty of time."

* * *

Rachel, Elwyn and Karen Darwin left the building together. "If you come back to the station with us, I'll get a police officer to take you home," Rachel told her.

In silence, Karen climbed slowly into the back of the car. She looked older now, even more haggard. "You will catch him, won't you?"

"We intend to do our very best," Elwyn assured her. "Right now, the murder of your daughter is our number one case."

"I hope he gets locked up for the rest of his natural, doing that to a young girl. What harm did she ever do to anyone? Her only crime was to have that bastard Gilbert for a father."

That did it. Karen Darwin broke into floods of tears. All Rachel could do was pass her the box of tissues off her dashboard.

Rachel was grateful to be able to hand the woman over to Arran Copeland. "Get her home safe and make sure she's all right. Make her a cup of tea when you get there. She's a recovering addict and I don't want to be responsible for her slipping back into her old ways."

With Karen safely on her way home, the pair made their way upstairs to be greeted by a long-faced Jonny holding a cold compress to one of his eyes.

"Bloody creep lamped me one."

"Who? Jack Fairhurst?" Rachel asked in surprise. "He didn't strike me as violent."

"Believe me, he's got some temper. He certainly wasn't for coming in of his own accord. In the end it took three of us to even cuff him."

"Is the eye bad?" Elwyn asked.

"I'll mend. Amy put some special balm on it and reckons it won't go black. I hope not. I'm off out at the weekend with my new girlfriend. I don't want her getting the wrong impression."

Hearing her name Amy looked up from her desk. "Right set-to the pair had. But our Jonny got the better of him — eventually. Oh, and Dotty told me Mary Dunn did know who Fairhurst was and didn't approve of his relationship with Kimberley. She knew his family, apparently. Said they were bad stock."

"We'd better get him interviewed, see what's going on," Rachel said. She turned to Elwyn. "Speaking of girlfriends, how's it going with Tina?"

"She's looking for work like I said but she's not getting anywhere."

"What's she doing for money?" Though Rachel knew what was coming. "She's asked you, hasn't she?"

"Last night, over supper," he admitted. "She asked me for five grand."

"Elwyn, you can't! You hardly know the woman. Give into her now and she'll be back for more."

Elwyn looked doubtful. "I feel for her, Rachel. It's a tough world out there and it isn't as if I'm not in a position to help."

Rachel had to do something to stop him. Something about Tina just didn't feel right. "Don't do anything yet, stall her until we've got more information."

"You can't go investigating her, Rachel. That wouldn't be right."

"Just a little background information. It can't do any harm, and then you'll know for sure if she's on the level or not."

"Okay, but just a light touch," he agreed. "Her full name is Tina Barrett, she's thirty-five and lives in Stockport. The estate agents she worked for was Hammonds."

"I'll make it a priority and get back to you before we finish for the day," she promised. "Now, let's get on with interviewing Fairhurst. I'll see him in a different light knowing he just punched one of my team. He's not quite the gentle soul he makes himself out to be."

CHAPTER THIRTY-NINE

Rachel and Elwyn found Jack Fairhurst and the duty solicitor in an interview room, deep in conversation.

"You attacked one of my officers," Rachel began. "Why'd you do that?"

Fairhurst shrugged. "Didn't like his attitude. Stuck-up, know-it-all prat, coming to the house and dragging me outside like that."

"Well, you haven't done your case any good. For starters we now know you have a temper. You kept that one under wraps."

Fairhurst glowered at Rachel and shook his head. "So what? Stupid police, you have nothing better to do than pick on innocent folk."

"But are you innocent, Mr Fairhurst?" Elwyn asked. "Only we've received certain information that suggests otherwise."

Fairhurst jumped to his feet. "What information? Someone been telling tales, have they? Who?"

"No one," Rachel said. "Calm down or we'll get nowhere. We've got the results back on forensic tests run on certain items we found. Cigarette ends and an empty lager can came back with your DNA on them."

Fairhurst looked puzzled. "So, I smoke and I like a drink. Like a lot of other people."

"We found these items in the crypt at St Paul's Church. Alongside the body of a murdered girl. Would you like to explain how that happened?"

Fairhurst looked first at his solicitor and then at Rachel. "I've never been in any crypt. I didn't even know the place had one. This is some sort of set up. Has to be." He turned to his solicitor. "This lot just want to pin the murder on someone and I fit the bill."

"Nothing of the sort, Mr Fairhurst," Rachel said. "Your DNA on those items points to you being in that crypt. Perhaps you'd like to tell us what happened, what part you played in the killing of Emma Gilbert."

"I don't even know the girl and I certainly had nothing to do with her death. Like I said, I've been set up, if not by you then by someone else. Think about it, it's easy enough to collect a few fag ends and an empty beer can. Make some of those enquiries you're so fond of, then make the real killer talk." Fairhurst glared at them.

"There was a time when I might have gone for that," Rachel told him. "But since then, you've showed your true colours, attacked one of my team. You're a violent man, Jack Fairhurst, that's the truth of the matter, isn't it?"

"No, no, you've got it all wrong. He made me angry. I just hit him on the spur of the moment. He wouldn't listen. I needed to make a call, tell Kim where I was going, but he refused. He said there was no time and that we had to leave right away. He kept on and on, and then I just saw red, lashed out." He shook his head. "That's not like me at all, and I'm sorry."

Rachel wasn't sure whether to believe him or not. To date, he hadn't lied to them but there was something not quite right there, something that had bothered Mary too. "You've known Kimberley for some time, haven't you?"

"I've known her for years. Well, you'll probably find out so I'll tell you. We were an item a long time ago, twenty years or more now. We were going to get wed in fact. But I did the dirty on her, started seeing another woman and she dumped me. After that I ran off to Europe with my mate to look for work. I didn't contact Kim at all for several years. Don't ask me why, scared of getting tied down, I suppose."

"I believe your behaviour didn't impress Mary," Rachel said.

"She warned me off. Mary made no secret of how she felt. But we'd been getting on these last months, she'd begun to trust me again."

"You see, if Mary did disapprove and she persuaded Kimberley to dump you, it might be construed as a motive for murder."

Fairhurst stared at her. "But she didn't. Me and Kim are solid. Oh, the old biddy tried but that doesn't mean I did her any harm. You can't pin the two murders on me if that's your game? I've never harmed a fly, and I certainly wouldn't kill a defenceless old woman and a young girl."

Something about his demeanour told Rachel that he was speaking the truth. And he was right, it would be a simple matter to set him up.

"D'you know a man known on the street as 'Ghost'?"

"Oh, him. Yeah, I have heard people mention that name. They wonder if he really exists. He's become a legend, a — what d'you call it — a myth. At least that's what that vicar says."

"Henry Neville? You've discussed Ghost with him?"

"Not really, just in passing. He asked me if I knew him. Like I said, the man's a mystery."

Rachel made a note to ask Neville herself. "Okay, suppose for one minute that we go along with your story about being set up. Who do you know who'd do a thing like that to you? Who'd want to implicate you in murder?"

"Well, that doesn't take a genius to work out, does it? The real murderer. I reckon it has to be someone who knows me, and that someone was Kim's son, Ronan. That lad's got some right dodgy friends."

Rachel didn't know what to think. There could be some truth in what he was saying. "Okay, we'll investigate. But if you're lying to me, Jack Fairhurst, we'll have you arrested and charged with murder."

"So, can I go home now? Kim will be worried about me."

"No, I'm afraid not. You'll be staying with us until I've checked your story and had another look at Ronan Dunn."

* * *

Rachel and Elwyn returned to the incident room. "We're hanging on to Fairhurst while we check out some of what he's told us," Rachel told the team. "Amy, find out what Ronan Dunn's been up to of late. I need a word with that young man."

"What Fairhurst gave us was basically a sob story," Elwyn argued. "I mean, what more do we need? His DNA is on those items, it's plain enough to me."

"But he's right, Elwyn," Rachel said. "They could have been picked up and planted. I want us to be as sure as we can be that we've not missed anything."

Rachel disappeared into her office, sat down at her desk and groaned at the amount of paperwork littering it. She was tired and really couldn't be bothered right now. No matter what Kenton said, it would have to wait.

Instead, she googled Hammond, the estate agent, to find the phone number. She'd give them a ring before she went home, see if she could find out anything about Tina. The young woman who answered sounded friendly enough, so Rachel decided to try her luck. This was unofficial, so Rachel didn't say she was police.

"I'm trying to find a friend of mine who works with you," she began. "Tina Barrett. We lost touch and I want to invite her to a do I'm having."

"She's not here anymore, love. Not after what she did."

"Not been up to her old tricks again, has she?" Rachel said. "She promised too, said this job was right for her and she wouldn't muck it up."

"It wasn't that she couldn't do the job, she was great at it. It was chasing the boss and getting him to lend her a load of money that did it. His wife went mental. Then Tina disappeared. He's never going to get his money back. Tina's probably moved on to fleece some other poor sod."

"Oh dear. I thought she'd stopped all that. Poor man. She can be very persuasive. A lot of money, was it?"

"Five grand. He should have known better, that's all I can say. He was well and truly taken in. The idiot didn't even go to the police, which I would have done in his shoes."

Rachel's heart sank. "So, you don't know where she is then."

"No, but she'd better keep out of Alec's way. He's furious and won't hold back."

"Okay. I'll just have to keep looking. Thanks for the information."

Rachel put the phone down and buried her head in her hands. It was no good, she'd have to tell Elwyn. Catching sight of him through the glass door of her office, she beckoned to him.

"I've been on the phone to Hammonds. Your lady friend fleeced the boss out of five grand and then did a runner."

Elwyn didn't say a word. He simply turned and left the office. It was pointless going after him, what could she say?

Rachel was getting her stuff together ready to leave for the day, when Amy stuck her head round the door.

"The patrols are looking for Ronan Dunn. So far they've checked all his usual haunts but no luck, and Arlo Bain appears to have gone to ground too."

"I'll have a word with Ronan's mother tomorrow. See if she can help. As for Arlo, we needn't worry too much about him."

She was almost ready for the off when Rachel remembered that she hadn't spoken to Jude about the tracking device. "An extra layer of protection," she told her friend. "I disappear and am easily found. Has to help."

"And I've got just the thing. Looks like a watch and you charge it from the battery. Pop in tomorrow and I'll give it you."

Rachel smiled. Provided no one kidnapped her tonight, she had it sorted.

CHAPTER FORTY

The journey home was the usual slog. There were road works, which meant several detours, temporary traffic lights and slow-moving traffic. It was gone eight by the time she pulled into her lane. She was too tired to cook, so she resorted to a ready meal from the freezer. After that, a quick shower and bed.

She wanted an early start the following morning. They had to find Ronan Dunn and determine if there was anything in what Fairhurst had said.

An hour after arriving home she was propped up in bed, reading through her notes. There was something she wasn't seeing, and she knew why. The spectre of her long absence in Wales loomed large.

Tossing her notebook on the bedside table, she picked up her mobile and rang Belinda. "How'd it go?"

"No problems, but you should know that I kept Mia at home. I rang the school and she'd got plenty to do. I didn't want to take any risks with her safety."

"Thanks. Good thinking. I'm not aware of anything going on but it's better to be safe than sorry."

"Alan is enjoying having them here, even Len, despite him being such a noisy little bundle."

"I owe you both. Really, Belinda, I don't know what I would have done. Is Sofia settling?"

"Yes, she hasn't put a foot wrong and she's a great help."

That was something at least. After finishing the call, Rachel decided to call it a day and get some sleep. One last walk around the house, ensure it was locked up tight. There should be a couple of officers lurking outside somewhere. Rachel peered through all the windows but could see no sign of them.

She was in the hallway, about to go back upstairs, when she heard cutlery rattling in the kitchen drawer. She froze, her heart in her mouth. Why had she left speaking to Jude about the tracker until now? Rachel was convinced there was someone else in the house. Could it be the men who'd taken Sofia and Len? If they took her, how would she be found?

"Who's there?" she called. "Come out and show yourself." Rachel had her mobile in her dressing-gown pocket, finger poised on the quick dial number for the station. Where were those officers? She was just considering dashing outside when she heard a cough.

"Why so edgy, Rachel? That's not like you. And where are the kids?" The deep voice issuing from the kitchen filled her with a mixture of relief and horror. What was he doing here? "Thought I'd tidy up while you had your shower. This place could do with a damn good clean."

Rachel marched into the kitchen. "You frightened me to death."

"I've never seen you so nervous. What's happened to you?"

"Never mind. Just answer the question. Why are you here?"

"I wanted to see you and the kids. I miss you all. Nothing sinister, just a dad craving a bit of family life."

Rachel stared at the suntanned man before her, hardly able to believe her eyes. This was the last thing she'd expected. When he'd left, Jed McAteer was running from the law, charges of illegal moneylending and possible murder hanging over his head, which he'd brought on his own head thanks to his involvement with the murderous Trio gang, led by Grace Blackmore.

"The kids are in danger, so I've put them somewhere safe." She glanced through the French doors into the garden. "You can't be seen here either. There are police officers watching the house. They see you and it won't end well."

"I've done nothing wrong, Rachel, whatever you think I'm guilty of."

The same old story. Did he really think she'd fall for it again? "So, why run then?"

"The burden of proof was stacked against me. Grace Blackmore saw to that. Need I say more?"

"So why didn't you stay? Why not work with the police and clear your name?"

Jed shook his head. "No chance. And anyway, I've got a new life now and I'm earning a damn good living. There's plenty for all of us, which is why I'm here."

"This good living. Legal, is it?"

"Yes, and I want you and the kids to come and join me. I've got a house near the coast, just north of Marbella. There's plenty of room and the weather's great. Len and the girls would love it. There are plenty of expats so they won't be lonely."

"I have a job," Rachel said. "Megan's at university and Mia is in an important year at school. Even if I wanted to, there's no way we can just up sticks and leave."

"Come on. You hate your job. You never used to but something's changed. You're tired. It's written all over your face. I reckon it's all become too much and you're looking for a way out. You can't kid me, Rachel. I know you too well. In bed at this hour? That's not you, Rachel."

What was the use of denying it? He'd read her correctly as he always did. "You're right in some of what you say. I do need a change, but no way am I going to run away to Spain with a known criminal. Think about it, Jed. I'd be giving up everything and everyone here to live with a man on the run. That is too big a price to pay for a bit of sunshine."

"There's me too," he said. He bent forward and gave her a peck on the cheek. "Think it through. I'll give you a day or so, and then I'll be in touch."

Rachel desperately needed a cup of tea. She turned her back to fill the kettle. When she moved around to speak to him again, Jed had gone. The curtains at the French window were open and the outside lights had come on. She heard someone banging on the front door.

A uniformed officer stood there. "You okay, ma'am? Me and my partner will take a wander round, but I think the back lights must have been triggered by a cat, or perhaps a fox."

A fox. They were right on that one. Rachel nodded. "Yes, we get a lot of foxes, it's the woods at the back. No worries, everything is fine." With a final goodnight, she locked up again. She needed to sleep, though thoughts of Jed and his offer would probably keep her tossing and turning all night. Given how she felt about the job and the other aspects of her life, was it something she should consider?

CHAPTER FORTY-ONE

Tuesday

The following morning Rachel got ready for work, the previous night's events crowding everything else from her mind. What had happened seemed so improbable that Rachel wondered if it had all been a dream. Wishful thinking. Jed's visit had been real enough, and although she hated herself for even considering it, as things were right now his offer was tempting. She pushed it aside. Something to mull over later when the day's work was done.

Rachel left early in order to miss the traffic, and for once enjoyed a reasonably quick ride in. She walked into the incident room to be met by a smiling Amy.

"We've found Ronan Dunn. Uniform is bringing him in now. Mind you, his mother is damned annoyed. She accused us of picking on the family, first her fella and now her son."

Kimberley was right, but upset her or not, Rachel had to get to the truth. "Put him in interview room two, and me and Elwyn will have a word."

"I wouldn't mind a go at him, ma'am," Amy said, following Rachel to her office door.

"We'll see."

Amy pointed to a package on Rachel's desk. "Jude dropped that off for you. She said to wear it like you would a watch and if anything happens, she'll do the rest."

It was the tracker, had to be. "Thanks, Amy, I'll speak to Jude in a minute. Later this morning, I want you and Jonny out looking for Arlo Bain. But hang on until Ronan's been interviewed."

Rachel went into her office, opened the package and put on the watch. It didn't look anything special. She rang Jude. "It looks just like a watch. Are you sure it'll work?"

"Positive, and it means I can find you anywhere. It's got GPS so I can track you with an app on my mobile."

"Sounds the business, thanks. I'll catch up with you later."

Tracker sorted, she went to find Elwyn. He was staring out of the incident room window, a mug of coffee in his hand.

Rachel showed him her watch. "I disappear, you contact Jude, she'll know what to do."

"Let's hope that doesn't become necessary. You get kidnapped they could kill you before we've had time to act."

Ever the voice of reason. "You've got that long face again. I don't know anyone who does moody like you, Elwyn. What's happened?"

"I tackled Tina about the money," he said, turning to face her. "Admitted it she did. Blatantly. And with a smile on her face. She reckoned if you hadn't stuck your nose in she'd have been somewhere in the sun by now. I can't believe the cheek of the woman."

Rachel rubbed his arm. "I'm sorry, Elwyn, but Tina was no good. I sensed it from the off. What sort of friend would I be if I'd just let you walk into it?"

He sighed. "I take your point, but it was good while it lasted."

"Right. You up for an interview with Ronan Dunn? Find out if he had a hand in planting that evidence in St Paul's crypt."

"You do know he'll deny it, don't you? Cheeky little sod is bound to. If he did plant it, it'll be on the say-so of some villain who'll have threatened him. When we eventually set him free, he's got to go back out there. I don't reckon much to his chances."

"In that case we'll have to protect him. If those cigarette ends and the can were down to him, we need to know. It's crucial to finding out who did take part in Emma's murder and who didn't."

* * *

Ronan Dunn appeared stunned. He sat in the interview room, his eyes darting from the man in the smart suit beside him and the officer in his uniform at the window. His mother, Kimberley, had been told and invited to come along but had refused.

"My client has made a statement," the solicitor said as Rachel and Elwyn entered the room. "It's all there, so he hasn't much more to say."

Rachel cast her eyes over the page and shook her head. "I hope he has, because there's a great deal missing. The bit about planting evidence, for one."

Ronan raised his eyes and stared at her, terrified.

"Have you been threatened, Ronan? Has someone said they'll hurt you if you speak to us?"

He shook his head and glanced at the solicitor.

"You see, if you are being leaned on, we can protect you." Rachel smiled. "We will make sure you're somewhere safe where no one can hurt you."

"They'll find me," he said with a shrug. "They know everything. I talk to you and they'll kill me."

"No, that won't happen," Rachel said. "I promise you'll be protected night and day. You have to trust me, Ronan."

"If I do — trust you, I mean — what d'you want from me?"

"I need to know about the cigarette ends and the empty beer cans in the crypt. I want you to tell me how they got there."

"Jack, I suppose."

"Jack Fairhurst? Why d'you say that, Ronan?"

He gave another shrug. "Well, he must have left them behind."

"Are you sure? You see, I think that's what you were told to say. But the truth is quite different, isn't it?"

"Don't know. It must have been Jack."

"Why d'you say that?"

Ronan looked down at his hands. "Word has it he killed that girl."

"That remains to be seen. You see, I don't believe Jack was ever in the crypt. I think that someone collected the evidence and put it where we'd find it. You know the sort of things — cigarette butts and an empty can Jack had drunk from. That someone knew we'd test them for DNA, find Fairhurst's and take it from there."

Ronan stared at Rachel. "You can't prove that. I've never been down there. It's all dark and spooky. I would never go into that crypt on my own."

"Be absolutely sure, Ronan, because if you have, there will be DNA traces and we will find them." She waited, giving him time. "Think about it, think about what your mother would want you to do. She's a good woman, Ronan, she's still grieving for her own mother. This is a murder case. You collude with whoever murdered that girl and you'll be in serious trouble. Surely, you don't want to have us chasing the wrong suspect?"

All at once, Ronan raised his hands and slapped them down on the table. "Okay, okay. It was me. I was told to collect that load of rubbish and scatter it round that girl." He pulled a face. "It was horrible. I've never seen a dead 'un before, turned my stomach it did. They said the same thing would happen to me if I said anything."

"Who, Ronan? Who told you to plant the stuff?"

"Ghost and his mate."

Rachel sighed. "I need his real name. Ghost won't do."

"I don't know his real name. Truth is, I don't know him at all. He only ever spoke to me over the phone. But he does have a mate who he works with."

"Does his mate have a name?"

Ronan shook his head. "I've no idea who he is. I've never even spoken to him."

"Okay, you haven't seen them face to face, but do you have any idea who they are? You're pretty streetwise, we know you deal drugs so you must know the villains on this patch."

Ronan gave Rachel a filthy look. "They're not Gilbert's people, I know that much. I was told not to let on to Arlo either. He's in Gilbert's pocket and Ghost didn't want his plan getting out."

"You are going to write another statement, a more comprehensive one. You will be staying here until I arrange for you to go to a safe house. I'll speak to your mum and tell her what's happening. Once you're there, you don't leave until we come and get you, understand?"

Ronan nodded. "Does this mean Jack's off the hook?"

"Yes, thanks to you."

CHAPTER FORTY-TWO

Rachel returned to the incident room and brought the team up to date. "Fairhurst was set up by the goons we're chasing. It might have worked too, if we didn't have our own opinion of the man."

"In all our dealings with him Fairhurst has seemed like an okay sort of chap," Jonny said. Apparently, he had no hard feelings about the black eye Fairhurst had given him.

"My thoughts exactly," Rachel said. "Young Ronan will need to go into a safe house for the duration. When they find out he's told us the truth, Ghost and his people will be after him. I'll get that organised and then we'll tell his mother." She looked at Jonny. "Any luck finding Arlo?"

"Not yet, but I'll pay a visit to his apartment, see if he's hiding out there."

"When you do find him, I want a word and it's important." Rachel disappeared into her office and spent the next ten minutes on the phone. She'd just finished when Amy knocked on her office door.

"Is there a problem?"

Amy gave her an odd look. "Lauren Gilbert is in reception asking for you. Elwyn offered to have a word but she refused. You or no one, she said."

"Okay, I'll go down in a moment. I want you to go round and speak to Kimberley Dunn. Tell her what's happening with her son and get some clothes and stuff for him. When that's organised, get an officer to drive him and someone from family liaison to the house."

"I'll sort it, ma'am."

* * *

Rachel had never met Lauren Gilbert. She had never even seen a photo of her. She knew Jacob was in his sixties and was surprised to see how much younger Lauren was.

She was in reception, pacing to and fro, her high heels clicking on the wooden floor. Rachel approached, to be met with a scowl and a torrent of abuse.

"I don't do waiting. I demand action. You've got to do something now, at once."

Rachel had no idea what she was on about, but it had to be important to make her so angry. "What's happened, Mrs Gilbert?"

Lauren was taller than Rachel, particularly in those heels. She stood glaring down at her. "My Jacob is missing. You have to find him."

"I can certainly try, Mrs Gilbert, but it depends on the circumstances. For instance, are you sure he wants to be found?"

"Don't be stupid. Something must have happened to him, and I'm worried sick."

Enraged would have been a more accurate description. If Jacob Gilbert hadn't gone walkabout, his disappearance could have something to do with the enmity between him and Ghost. But first, Rachel must rule out anything else. "Could he have gone to visit someone, a friend perhaps?"

Lauren gave her a withering look. "He hasn't left me, if that's what you're implying. Jacob loves me, loves our home and our life together. It's a lot to give up on a whim. Something has happened to him, I just know it."

"Okay, but perhaps he's simply taking a break. Has he taken any of his possessions — clothing? His passport?"

"No, all his stuff is at home where it should be."

Rachel had heard the gossip. Jacob's reputation as a womaniser was common knowledge. "You're quite sure he's not seeing a friend or gone away for a few days?"

"I know what you're thinking but you're wrong. Jacob has had his moments in the past but he's promised me things are different now, and I believe him." Lauren shook her head. "No, Detective, this is not about a woman, it's about something else entirely."

"Has anyone threatened him?" Rachel asked, knowing full well that the only person with the temerity to threaten Gilbert would be Ghost.

"No, but then if they had, Jacob wouldn't have told me. He doesn't like to worry me."

"Earlier this week we contacted you and asked if Mr Gilbert would come in and identify a murder victim who we now know to be his daughter. You said he wasn't available. Was he missing then?"

Lauren turned her back on Rachel and clattered off towards the window. "Yes. I didn't say anything then because I thought he'd be back, that he'd gone off for the day on business. As far as I'm aware he doesn't yet know that Emma is dead."

"What sort of business is your husband in, Mrs Gilbert?"

Lauren looked a little shamefaced. "I don't really know. He buys and sells things."

Rachel gave a little smile. "I'd say from your lifestyle he does it rather well."

Lauren was starting to get impatient again. "Look, are all these questions really necessary? I simply want him found. Surely, that can't be too difficult, even for you lot? He's well known around the city. He gives generously to a variety of community projects and he's often in the papers."

"How long has he been gone?"

"Four days." Lauren rummaged around in her handbag and took out her phone. "And then there's this." She handed

Rachel the phone. On the screen was a text. "It arrived yesterday. I've no idea who sent it, they probably used one of those burner phones."

It was a ransom demand, but it wasn't asking for money. Whoever had sent it was asking to meet with Lauren, or Jacob's business partner.

"It's a takeover, has to be," Lauren said. "They want in. But no way is that happening. Jacob would never allow it."

"Can I hang on to your mobile for a day or so?" Rachel asked.

Lauren nodded. "There's not much on it anyway. It's not the one I use for my personal stuff."

"Any more communication, or if your husband turns up, let us know straight away," Rachel said. "I'll get your phone to Forensics. They may be able to glean something from that text."

CHAPTER FORTY-THREE

Jonny rang Bain's doorbell but got no response. He tried calling through the letterbox. "Mr Bain! It's Jonny Farrell, I'd like a quick word."

Suddenly Bain flung the door open. "I thought I told you not to bother me again. I've said all you're getting, now go and do one."

Jonny merely shrugged. "No can do, I'm afraid, Mr Bain. You see, my boss wants a word urgently. She's got more questions for you."

"I get noticed by the wrong people and you lot will have a body on your hands," Bain said angrily. "I for one don't fancy ending up like that. All right, I'll meet your boss but it's on my terms."

"We can be discreet too," Jonny said. "The drug squad doesn't have the monopoly you know."

"I'll meet her in one hour in that little café behind the Printworks. Tell her to come alone and not to be late. I've got a meet afterwards that won't wait."

Jonny left him to it. Bain was an odd one, unlike any police operative he'd ever met. He supposed being undercover must bring its own problems, pretending to engage in villainy being one of them. Without letting Rachel know, he'd decided to hang around the venue, keep a wary eye on Bain and make sure everything went as it should. He couldn't put his finger on why, but Bain had him rattled. He didn't trust the man.

* * *

Rachel wrote a note on the incident board to say that Gilbert had gone missing. Elwyn read it over her shoulder. "It might be nothing," she said, "then again it might be of major importance. We suspect he's got a killer after his patch but I can't believe a man like Jacob Gilbert doesn't have people watching his back."

"These people — Ghost and his cronies — are clever. They've got us running round in circles," Elwyn said. "And we don't know that Gilbert doesn't know him, perhaps even as someone he thinks he can trust, one of his own dealers, for instance."

It was something to think about. Rachel realised she'd have to speak to Lauren again. The woman wasn't stupid, she must know more than she'd said about what her husband was up to, how he earned his money. If she wanted him back, she had no choice but to confide in them.

Meanwhile, Amy had been on the office phone. "That was Jonny, ma'am. He's arranged a meet for you with Arlo Bain." She scribbled down the details and handed them to Rachel. "Jonny says to tell you he's checking something out and he'll be back in later."

Rachel took the note and went to have a word with Kenton. Uppermost in her mind right now was Gilbert and what had happened to him. Kenton would have to know about him being missing and about the text. She'd be interested to have his take on what it meant.

"Elwyn, any calls I'll be back shortly, I need a word with the Super. After that I'm meeting with Bain. While I'm gone, would you go through what we've got on Gilbert, see if you can figure out where he might have gone. He may have a bolthole his wife isn't telling us about."

"Don't you think she'd have told us? And if his wife doesn't know, how are we supposed to?" he muttered.

Elwyn wasn't himself. He didn't usually suffer from moods but he was definitely in one at the moment. Rachel put it down to the Tina business. The fact that he'd been taken in so easily must have upset him, made him feel foolish. Rachel wanted to help but she had no idea where to start. She would have liked to invite him to hers for a meal but given that Jed could appear again at any time, she didn't dare.

She left the office and went to knock on Kenton's door. His desk was covered in paperwork, much like her own.

"It never ends," he said, looking up. "The ACC has asked for a report on the murders. He wants to know how we're doing and he didn't ask nicely. Sorry, Rachel, that means I'm going to have to push you."

"We're working as hard as we can, sir," she said, "chasing up every lead. But now we've got a distraction. I've just been told that Jacob Gilbert has disappeared. His wife came in this afternoon. On the one hand I'm quite relieved, on the other, it could mean trouble. He has a rival, a villain known on the streets as 'Ghost'. We suspect this Ghost of the murders we're currently trying to solve, including that of Emma Gilbert. When he hears of it, Jacob will want revenge."

"You've no idea where he might go?"

"His wife wasn't much help on that score. She's convinced he hasn't simply taken off and that there is something behind it. But Gilbert has a reputation as a womaniser. He could have met someone and be staying with them. Lauren's touchy on the subject, and won't admit what's staring her in the face."

"She could be right. But let's face it, Rachel, would it be such a loss if he never showed his face in these parts again?"

"That's not the point, sir. Gilbert has been missing for several days. There has been one threatening text message, so it's clear to me that Lauren suspects foul play. It is our duty to investigate."

"Okay, but don't let finding Gilbert divert you from your main task."

CHAPTER FORTY-FOUR

Rachel went to her meeting with Bain on foot. The air would do her good, clear her head. Kenton might not be concerned about what had happened to Gilbert, but she was. If he'd gone the same way as Mary and Emma, it would only add to their already heavy workload. Not that that would bother Kenton, he'd simply tell her and the team to get on with it.

The café was tiny. If you didn't know it was there you could easily miss it. It had the added advantage of tiny windows, so people walking past couldn't see who was inside.

"What now?" Bain began as soon as Rachel took her seat. "Only I doubt we've anything else to discuss."

"The girl, Sofia, the one who came to sell you a bag of heroin she'd stolen from Gilbert's house. At least, she told me you bought it from her."

Bain looked mystified. "She's lying. I might make a good show of working for Gilbert, but I have to draw the line somewhere. You've got this totally wrong. I don't deal heroin. That's just an act, my 'bad guy' persona."

He wasn't looking her in the eye, which to her said he was lying. "Sofia recalls it quite clearly. She knows you from your dealings with Gilbert. She remembered you visiting the Gilberts' house when she was working there. The night she stole the stuff and ran she contacted you, and then went to your apartment to broker the deal."

Bain shook his head. "Uh uh. That definitely didn't happen. It's not the sort of thing I'd do. The girl is telling fairy tales, lying through her teeth."

"Well, that's what she said. And I know this girl — she's reliable, eager to help us with our current case."

Bain glared at her, simmering with rage. "You're prepared to take the word of some illegal against that of a serving police officer, are you? Not a good idea, love. It'll be bound to upset Superintendent Swain if he hears of it."

He was obviously struggling to keep his temper under control. Rachel had to cool things down if she was to get anything out of him. "It's not the heroin that interests me but something else that was in the bag."

"You're not listening. How many times do I have to tell you? There was no girl, and there was certainly no bag of heroin."

"Perhaps you've forgotten. Sofia is from Eastern Europe, she's slim, pretty and has dark hair."

"No, still doesn't ring any bells," he insisted. "What's with this other something you're after?"

"It could be important evidence. It was a lock of hair in a black velvet bag and I need to know what happened to it."

Bain got to his feet. "Sorry, can't help, and don't contact me again. Every time I speak to you my position is compromised still further. It's vital to this operation that I remain incognito, and I'm not willing to risk blowing my cover."

Bain turned his back on her and stalked out of the café.

* * *

Meanwhile, Jonny had been hanging around in a shop doorway that had a view of the café entrance. He saw Bain leave and decided to follow, reasoning that it could do no harm to see where he went.

Rachel left shortly after Bain. Jonny waited until she was out of sight and then took off after Bain. He half expected

Bain to take a taxi back to his apartment, but he walked on. Seeing that this could take some time, Jonny sent Elwyn a quick text to tell him what he was doing. A call would have been quicker but he didn't want to argue the toss. Elwyn might well have told him to go back to the station. He followed Bain across the busy road onto Shudehill and on towards the cathedral.

Having crossed the open space onto Victoria Street, Bain hung around for a few seconds, watching. For a moment Jonny thought he might have been spotted and ducked behind a huge tub full of shrubs. Seconds later, an old estate car pulled up and Bain got into the passenger seat.

From his hiding place, Jonny tried to get a look at the driver but the sun was reflecting off the windscreen. He could just make out Bain and the other man deep in conversation. After a while, things seemed to get heated. Suddenly, Bain was waving his fists at his companion. Was this man another dealer? Someone connected to Gilbert? Jonny had no way of knowing. All he could do was write down the registration number.

Jonny was just about to leave them to it when Bain jumped out of the car. He stuffed his hands into his pockets and began to cross back over the open space onto Victoria Street. This meant that Bain would pass right by where he was hiding. Jonny dared not move. All he could hope for was that Bain had other things on his mind and wouldn't notice him. Hunkered down, fingers crossed, Jonny held his breath while Bain passed on the other side of the planter. He was just about to breathe again when someone whispered in his ear.

"Covert work's not for you, mate. Your skills just aren't up to it."

Bain.

"What's your game, pretty boy? Protecting the lady copper, eh? Not much good though, are you?"

Jonny tried a chuckle. It wasn't convincing. "Just curious. I wondered who your other meet was with."

"If you're that interested in my work and the world I move in, why not come and join me?"

Jonny wasn't stupid. This wasn't about an undercover officer offering an insight into his world, far from it. This was Bain making sure Jonny didn't get in his way. "And if I refuse?"

He felt something hard press into the small of his back.

"In case you're wondering, it's a revolver, so no sudden moves. Just walk nice and easy until we're out of here."

"You can't do this," Jonny said. "You're a police officer just like me."

"Not quite like you, mate. I've got more sense. I saw my chance and I took it."

In that instant, Jonny knew his instinct about Bain had been right. The man was no detective working undercover for the drug squad, he was a crook. But was Bain a murderer too? "What d'you mean, saw your chance?"

"To make some real money, not the pittance this game pays." Bain pressed the weapon harder into Jonny's back. "Don't tell me you've never been tempted, we're all human."

Jonny didn't answer. He was busy trying to work out how to extricate himself from this mess. "Look, you don't want to do this. We can talk, do a deal. What do you say?"

Bain laughed. He shoved Jonny forward. "See that taxi parked over there? We're going to get in it. You will keep your big mouth shut or you won't like the consequences."

"Where are we going?"

"Where you can do no more harm."

As they walked, Jonny looked for the estate car but it had gone. "Your mate didn't hang around."

"He wasn't a mate and it's got nothing to do with you. Keep asking stupid questions and I'll finish you for good. Be warned, I've a real temper, and I've got rid of people before."

Jonny felt sick. This was as bad as it got. He wondered how the team would find him — if they ever did. They were a clever and resourceful bunch but it would be like looking for a needle in a haystack.

CHAPTER FORTY-FIVE

Rachel had returned to the station and was on the phone to Belinda, partly to check on the kids but also to have a word with Sofia. Bain had been positive that he hadn't taken delivery of the drugs and the other stuff, but Rachel didn't believe him.

"Sofia, when you left the Gilbert's house you needed money. Is that right?"

"Yes, I told you. I went to this man I know, Arlo Bain. He lives in one of those new apartment blocks in Ancoats and does business with Gilbert."

"And he took the bag with everything in it and gave you cash in return?"

"Yes. I had thought I'd keep the crucifix but he said it was valuable, and would give me another couple of hundred if I sold that as well."

"And you're sure it was Bain, not someone else?"

"Yes, I knew him from Gilbert's house. He used to chat me up. Said if I ever needed help, I should find him. He even gave me a card with his address on it," Sofia said.

So, Bain had lied to her. Why? The reason was simple enough, he was not what he said. Arlo Bain was a bent copper, had to be. "Do you still have that card, by any chance?"

"I may have. I'll have a look later when Len is in bed, and if I find it, Alan will bring it over."

"Thanks, Sofia, that's very helpful."

Elwyn and Amy were in the incident room but there was no sign of Jonny. Shame, she wanted to run this one past the entire team. She left her office and went to join them. "I've got something to put to you," she said. "I think Arlo Bain is bent, creaming money off the top of deals when the opportunity presents itself. Like with Sofia for instance. He denies all knowledge of her taking drugs to him. Besides the heroin, she also sold him a valuable piece of jewellery stolen from Lauren Gilbert and the lock of hair belonging to Lauren's brother. He's drug squad, so it would be an easy matter for him to hand in the lot."

"I thought he was dodgy when we first set eyes on him," Amy said. "I didn't like him much either."

"You spoke to him about this?" Elwyn asked.

"Yes. I wanted to know about the lock of hair. It's important to our case. It ended up in the hands of someone who knew how they could use it to mess up our investigation into Mary's murder."

"And you think that was Arlo Bain," Elwyn said. "D'you want to bring him in?"

"I think we've got to. But what I want to know is who Bain passed that lock of hair to. We know that when Mary was murdered, he was in custody in Anglesey. Has anything come back from Jude yet on that carrier bag and gun?"

Amy checked the system. "No. She must still be working on them."

Rachel rang her. "Jude, we need results from those remaining items from the crypt. I'm desperate. We now have a person of interest and I want evidence to nail him."

"The gun has been wiped clean, or else whoever used it was wearing gloves. The bag has been kicking around for a while. There are multiple prints on it, most of them smudged, so not much use, I'm afraid. Sorry if you'd built your hopes up, but disappointment was always on the cards."

"Do we have anything else?"

"I'm afraid not. I suppose we could take another look in that crypt. As you know, we've been through it once and gathered what we considered the main items of evidence, but the place was so dirty and messed up, things could have been missed."

"Would you do that? You could find just what we need. There has to be something, and I really want to nail this one. Neither Mary nor Emma deserved what was done to them. And who's to say it will stop with those two? Ghost is hellbent on taking over Gilbert's patch, and only today we learned that Gilbert is missing."

"We'll be there first thing in the morning. If there is the merest scrap of evidence, we'll find it."

Jude sounded so positive but Rachel had her doubts. "Where's Jonny?" she asked the team.

"He went out shortly after you, ma'am," Amy said.

"Did he say where to?"

"No. I'll ring him."

Rachel headed to the coffee corner and switched the kettle on. She needed to think, go over what Bain had told her and consider what it meant.

"His phone is dead, ma'am," Amy said. "He must have forgotten to charge it. That's not like him I must say."

No, it wasn't, and for reasons she couldn't explain it sent a shiver down Rachel's spine. "Elwyn, get onto Communications and find out when Jonny last used his mobile and his position."

"It's okay he's sent me a text," Elwyn said, checking his own mobile. "Apparently, he went off to keep an eye on you when you met up with Bain and then he followed the man. He wanted to know where he was going and who he was meeting up with after you." He passed the phone to Rachel.

"I can hardly read it," she complained.

"It's our sort of shorthand," Elwyn explained.

"Jonny shouldn't have done that. He could get himself into all sorts of bother. Bain was in a foul mood when he left me. If he caught sight of Jonny, it wouldn't go down well."

"Shall I get onto CCTV? Take a look at that part of the city?" Elwyn said.

"The office is only round the corner. I'll go and see them myself." She beckoned to Elwyn. "You too. I want Jonny finding, and urgently."

CHAPTER FORTY-SIX

The area surrounding the cathedral, close to Victoria Station and Exchange Square with all its expensive shops, was a busy part of the city. Rachel and Elwyn sat for several minutes, watching dozens of people going about their lives, oblivious of the cameras watching them.

"Look." Elwyn pointed towards the Printworks. "That's Bain coming out of the front entrance. And that's you, heading off towards Deansgate."

"But where's Jonny?" Rachel asked shuffling her chair closer to the screen.

"There," Elwyn said. "He's behind Bain and — there he is — he's stopped. That must be when he sent me the text."

The pair watched as Bain headed towards the cathedral then across the open ground of the square.

"If Bain turns round, Jonny's scuppered," Elwyn said. "Good boy, he's ducked down behind the large planter."

They saw Bain get in the estate car, and the ensuing argument between him and the driver. "Can we get the registration number?"

The CCTV operative nodded. "I'll get the frame blown up."

"Hang on. Bain's on the move again." Elwyn pointed.

Rachel grabbed hold of Elwyn's arm. "He's seen Jonny. Look, the two of them are talking."

Elwyn chuckled. "Wouldn't you like to be a fly on the wall?"

But Rachel wasn't smiling. "Something's not right. See the way they're walking towards that taxi? Jonny looks stiff, he keeps looking round like he's afraid of something."

Elwyn craned his neck. "I can't be sure but I suspect Bain has a knife or gun pressed into Jonny's back." He turned to the operative. "Get that frame blown up too, will you?"

Rachel's stomach churned. This was as serious as it got. If Elwyn was right, one of her officers could well be in mortal danger. "That taxi," she barked, "we need its registration and owner. I want to know where Bain took Jonny and I want to know quick. His life is in danger."

* * *

The pair returned to the station to await the enlarged frames. They found Amy in the incident room, Kenton standing over her.

"You have a problem, DC Metcalfe tells me."

"Jonny Farrell has been kidnapped by Arlo Bain. We've just seen CCTV film which shows Bain leading Jonny away with what looks like a weapon pressed into his back."

Kenton waved a hand dismissively. "He's in no danger. Bain is undercover drug squad. This will be some sort of show for the people he's currently trying to impress. DC Farrell will be back among us in no time."

Rachel was running out of patience. Why couldn't Kenton see what was staring him in the face? "I don't think so, sir. This is for real. Bain is bent, I've had my suspicions about him from the start."

"Rubbish. Just to reassure you, I'll have a quick word with Swain. How's that?"

As he left the office, Rachel turned to Elwyn. "He's a bloody idiot. How can he not see what's going on?"

"Because he's not working the case," Elwyn said. "From where he's standing it's a simple matter of believing whatever gives him a quiet life."

"How are we going to help Jonny?" Rachel asked. "Do we bring Bain in? Tell him what we suspect, that we know what he's up to?"

Elwyn shook his head. "If he is holding Jonny, he's not likely to tell us, is he? And it could make things worse. No, more important than arresting Bain is finding Jonny safe and sound." He sighed. "Any chance we could get a warrant, search that apartment of his?"

The question hung in the air as Kenton returned. "Swain assures me that all is well with Bain," he told them. "In fact, he finds it ludicrous that you could even entertain the notion that his man could be bent. He's spoken to Bain, who told him he did see DC Farrell earlier. They exchanged a few words and Farrell left for the station safe and well."

"We can see from the CCTV that that's not what happened," Rachel argued. "Jonny was being marched off somewhere and he didn't look happy."

Amy had overheard, and got straight on the phone to ring him. "Jonny's phone is still dead, ma'am."

"He'll have forgotten to switch it on," Kenton said dismissively as he left them to it.

"See what we're up against," Rachel snapped. "I don't believe a word of it. Something is very wrong."

"Anyone got any suggestions?" Elwyn asked. "Do we approach Bain ourselves?"

"Where would that get us?" Rachel said. "We can't just go and ask him to please give our Jonny back. He's a professional and as hard as nails. He's not going to admit to anything, nor is he going to let his guard down. We need evidence, Elwyn, and I'm not sure where we can get it."

"You could tell Bain you've spoken to Sofia again and are having doubts about what she told you. Ask if he has any idea what might have happened to the heroin, whether it ended up on the street and who is likely to have bought it and sold it on."

"You mean pretend to get him onside?"

Elwyn nodded. "Play to his ego. Bain likes to think he's the expert around here, the one who's got everyone jumping to his tune."

"I'd struggle to make it real. What I really want to do is get that warrant you spoke about and tear his place apart."

Elwyn shook his head. "Can't happen, not with Kenton and Swain in his corner."

"You're right, we have to do something. Standing helplessly by won't get Jonny back. I want Bain watching." Rachel looked at Amy. "Get that organised. We need a couple of officers at that apartment block he lives in for starters. I want to know where he goes and who he speaks to. I want every movement and conversation logging. You see to that, Elwyn. Meanwhile, I'll ring Bain and then I'll go and see Jude. I need to speak to her in person, impress upon her how important it is to get the evidence she's currently processing."

Rachel didn't want to do this but what choice did she have? Kenton wouldn't help and neither would Bain's superiors. She took out her mobile and made the call.

"What're you bothering me for now?" he snapped. "I told you we're finished. Don't you understand English?"

"I owe you an apology," she said, making a face. "Since we met earlier I've spoken to Sofia again and I now know that she was lying. She was good, I'll give her that, but it's obvious to me now that she can't actually recall what happened to the stuff she stole from the Gilbert house."

"Good to know, but why ring me?"

"Because I need your help. I really need to find out what happened to that lock of hair. If Sofia didn't bring what she stole to you, I'd like to know who else she could have approached. Local dealers, people who'd be happy to cut a deal with her. There'll be no comeback, I'm simply after information from them."

"Sorry, no can do," he said, sounding a bit calmer. "I put you onto any of my contacts and that's my cover blown. You're on your own, love. Sort it yourself."

"All you have to do is show me where they hang out. You can just point out who Sofia might have known from her time in Gilbert's house."

"None of the dealers will talk to you, and I'm not prepared to risk my own safety."

"So, you're refusing to help. Even though this is a murder case."

"Nothing to do with me. Stop whining and find your own way out of the mess you're in."

CHAPTER FORTY-SEVEN

Jonny Farrell came to in utter blackness, as if he'd been blinded. Unable to see a thing, he had no idea where he was or what had happened. He groaned. He felt dreadful, every muscle in his body ached, particularly his shoulders, but he didn't know why. He felt sick, he had a thumping headache.

After a while, Jonny realised he was sitting on a concrete floor, his back against a wall. His arms were bound together behind his back, as were his ankles. He wondered if he'd been put in the crypt like the dead girl, but the smell, though unpleasant, wasn't the same.

He tried calling out. "Hello! Anyone there?"

Silence. Not even the sound of traffic, which was odd, given he'd last been in Manchester city centre.

He tried to wriggle free but whoever had tied him up had done a damn good job. Bain, he presumed. He seemed to remember having been with Bain before he'd blacked out.

Jonny closed his eyes. He needed to think, find a way to get free. The cord round his wrist and ankles was beginning to hurt and he was cold. He knew the team would try their best to find him — if they even knew he was missing. If they did, he reasoned, they'd be looking at CCTV. They'd know his last position from the text he'd sent Elwyn.

Given the headache, he guessed Bain had cracked him one. He had a vague recollection of looking up and seeing the tower block where Bain lived. Was that where he was? He had no way of knowing.

As his eyes became accustomed to the dark, Jonny made out the bulky shadows of what could be machines, or maybe furniture. Was he in a storeroom then? If there'd been windows there should be some light around them but the darkness was unremitting. So maybe he was in the crypt?

If Bain didn't come back, if his plan was to leave him here, Jonny knew he'd have a struggle surviving. He had no food or water and the temperature was dropping all the time.

He wriggled his fingers trying to get one hand free. They were definitely tied with rope — better than plastic. Jonny gave it several minutes of effort before he slumped, exhausted, onto his side. First sleep, and then he'd have another go.

* * *

Rachel left the station intending to go and see Jude. She pulled out into the main road and drove for a hundred metres or so when the car behind her flashed its headlights. She swore and drove on but the car followed, sticking close on her tail. After half a mile or so, it suddenly ploughed into her car, knocking it sideways. If she hadn't steered into the swerve, Rachel would have ploughed into the oncoming traffic. Angry and shaken, she pulled into the nearest lay-by, intending to sort out this maniac.

As the car pulled in behind her, Rachel realised she'd made a mistake. The man driving the other car was Arlo Bain.

"What the hell d'you think you're doing!" she yelled at him. "You could have got me killed."

He shrugged. "I've got a dealer who's prepared to chat if you're interested."

Rachel was about to give him another mouthful when she remembered Jonny. "Will it take long?"

"Why? Got somewhere to be?" He pointed to his passenger seat. "Get in. This'll be quick."

There was no time to ring the station, she could only do as she was told.

Bain set off at speed. "You're becoming a real pain, d'you know that? First that pretty boy of yours sticks his nose in, and now you." He grinned. "Well, you've seen the last of him. Now it's time to do something about you."

"You can't do this," Rachel said. She took her mobile from her pocket. "I'll have you arrested."

In one swift movement, Bain had snatched it from her hand and thrown it out of the window. "So much for that."

Rachel released her seatbelt, ready to jump for it the next time the car slowed down. In response, Bain took to the back streets of Ancoats, grabbed a handful of her hair and smashed her head into the dashboard. Momentarily stunned, she fell back into the seat.

Bain laughed. "Dear me, no airbag. I really must get this car sorted."

Dazed and sick, Rachel looked up. They had come to a halt outside his apartment block. Bain was saying something but the words were garbled, and she couldn't make it out.

Bain took her arm and dragged her into the building. They didn't go to his flat. Instead, they seemed to be in a dark corridor heading downwards. As in a dream, Rachel heard someone shout Bain's name. He answered but she couldn't make out what he said. Then the crunch of a metal door opening, and Bain shoved her forward into the pitch dark.

"I've got a visitor to see to. Stay here and don't get clever. I'll be back later to sort the pair of you."

As a parting shot, he grabbed her by the hair again and slammed her head against a concrete wall. Rachel crumpled like a rag doll.

CHAPTER FORTY-EIGHT

"Ma'am? Rachel! Is that you?"

Rachel heard a voice calling to her through the dark but couldn't make out what he — for it was a man — was saying. She'd no idea what had happened, or where she was. It was as if she were wandering, lost, in a dense fog.

"Rachel! It's me, Jonny. Is it really you? Are you okay?"

Jonny! Yes, of course, they were looking for Jonny. She opened her mouth to answer but the words stuck in her throat, and all she could do was groan.

"Speak to me, Rachel. I know it's you, I recognise that perfume you wear."

Perfume? What perfume? Rachel closed her eyes. Her head was throbbing and all she wanted to do was sleep.

"Wake up. We have to get out of here," Jonny called. "My hands and feet are tied, so I need your help."

She still couldn't make out what he was saying, though she was relieved to have found him. The team would be pleased too. The team? Where was the team? The team would find them. But where would they even start to look? She felt sick again.

"Rachel, we have to move, we don't have much time. If Bain comes back, he will kill us."

He seemed to be telling her something important, but Rachel couldn't work out what. She tried to sit up but the movement sent the room spinning. She recalled being with Bain in his car, and then . . . "He hit me," she said. "Where are you?"

"Over here. Follow my voice."

Rachel crawled along on her hands and knees until she felt him.

"I'm tied up. Anything you can do?"

Rachel tugged at the bonds around his ankles. "They're too tight, I can't undo them. A knife or something sharp would be handy. Jonny, I'm sorry but the best I can do is help you to your feet."

"You can barely stand yourself," he said.

"I just need my head to clear, then I'll be fine. That was quite some crack I took."

"We need to get a shift on. He comes back before we're ready to sort him and we won't stand a chance."

Rachel slowly struggled to her feet. The room spun again and she had to lean against the wall. She took a few deep breaths and tried to yank him up by the arms. "You're too heavy for me. Use the wall for leverage." She put her shoulder under his arm and tried to push him up.

Finally, after several minutes of effort, Jonny was on his feet. But given his ankles were tied, he had difficulty keeping his balance.

"There has to be a door somewhere," he said.

"How will we find it? It's pitch black in here."

"My key fob is in my pocket, there's a small torch on it."

Rachel rifled through his pockets and found it. "How does it work?"

"There's a button at one end, you just press it."

Rachel did so, and a thin beam of light pierced the dark. Three of the walls were made of concrete blocks but the fourth was metal. She nudged Jonny. "A door. It's big too. I reckon we're in a garage somewhere."

Rachel stumbled around, looking for something that might help them. If it was a garage there were certainly no tools, just furniture — an old sofa and several dining chairs. The sofa was covered with a tarpaulin. She snatched it off, intending to sit for a moment or two but recoiled in horror.

"Jonny! I think I've found Jacob Gilbert."

"Dead, is he?"

"Very much so. It looks as if the poor sod was tied up and left here to rot. He'd obviously been trying to get free of the rope around his wrists. They're rubbed raw."

"Any sign of what actually finished him off?"

"A bullet to the head," Rachel said soberly. "You're right, Jonny. We need to get out of here and fast. There's nothing to stop Bain from making sure we end up the same way."

"Try the door," he said.

Rachel banged on it with her fist. It held firm. She shone the feeble torch beam across it but couldn't see a handle, or a lock. "It's got to be one of those electronic jobs. I doubt we stand much chance of forcing it."

"We're running out of time, Rachel."

She rubbed her head. "Any ideas? Or do we just wait until he comes back and jump him?"

"Nice idea, but given the state the pair of us are in what are the chances we'll be successful? He'll have a gun, so we have to be spot on, whatever we try."

Jonny's words did nothing to make Rachel feel any better. Her head was reeling, her stomach churning. But sick as she was, their only chance was to give it their best shot.

They waited for Bain to return.

CHAPTER FORTY-NINE

Amy set down the receiver. "That was Jude on the phone. Rachel didn't turn up at the lab. What d'you reckon? Could she have gone somewhere else first?"

Elwyn looked up from his desk. He doubted it. Rachel was anxious to get whatever evidence Jude could offer in order to nail Bain. Something was wrong.

He called her mobile. "It's ringing but she's not picking up. Amy, get onto Comms and get a trace on Rachel's mobile — when it was last used and where it is now."

Elwyn checked the time. Rachel had left over an hour ago. City traffic allowing, the lab was only a ten-minute drive away. By now, she should have spoken to Jude and been back at the station.

He was considering this when the office phone rang. Arran Copeland picked up. Elwyn saw him nod and say, 'Okay.' Call over, Arran turned to them. "We could have a problem. DCI King's car has been found abandoned on a lay-by at that roundabout near the lab. There's no sign of the DCI."

Elwyn's mind was racing. "I want her car bringing in and going over by a forensic team. Tell them to check for any damage." He called Jude, and asked her if she'd seen Rachel at all that day.

"She's not been near," Jude said.

Elwyn told her what had happened. "We need to find her quick. Rachel told me about the tracker you gave her. Will it help?"

"Within a certain radius, yes. I'll give it a go and get back."

Kenton wouldn't like it but he had to be told. Apart from which, the time had come to stop putting off getting that warrant. Elwyn picked up the office phone and rang Kenton's office. "DCI King is missing, sir. She left for the hospital but her car's been spotted abandoned, and she's not answering her mobile."

"Turned on, is it?"

"Yes, sir. And I know Rachel. If she could answer, she would."

"What are you thinking?" Kenton said.

"That Bain has taken her too, sir."

"Him again. I swear, DS Pryce, you're obsessed."

"Nothing else makes any sense. Bain knew Rachel no longer believed in his drug squad story. She was convinced he was the guilty party in all this."

"And that makes him a kidnapper, does it? You have no evidence and your logic is flawed. Bain is police, like us. He does *not* go around kidnapping fellow officers."

"The warrant, sir?"

"No. Go and speak to him if you must, and be polite, but you haven't got enough for a search of his property."

Elwyn shook his head. Kenton had no idea. "Jude fitted Rachel with a tracking device. She's checking out the signal now and will get back."

"I suppose it's a case of find DCI King and you'll find DC Farrell. I presume you think they've both fallen foul of Bain?"

"I believe so, sir."

"See where the tracker takes you and ring me. Based on the outcome, I'll decide about the warrant."

That was something at least. Elwyn finished the call and addressed the team. "Kenton's not keen on us going after Bain, but that's what we're going to do. We haven't time to

205

hang about waiting for the paperwork either. Amy, Arran and you two." He nodded at the uniformed officers standing by the door. "We'll start at Bain's apartment."

Amy held out the office phone for him. "Jude, sir."

"The tracker I gave Rachel is a GPS one, so it has a long range. Currently, she's in Ancoats. Bengal Street."

"I knew it," Elwyn exclaimed. "Bain has her. Right. Let's get going."

He hadn't even thought to hang up the phone, so Jude overheard. "I'll meet you there," she said. "Just in case there are any technical issues."

* * *

Elwyn and the others stood outside the apartment block, looking up. "What now, sir? Do we go and knock on his door?"

"No, Amy. We wait until Jude gets here and see if she can pinpoint exactly where Rachel is."

Amy pointed to the small saloon pulling up behind them. Jude got out and pointed down the side of Bain's block. "The signal is strong here," she muttered, walking up and down a small area of footpath. "Something's wrong. According to the tracker, she should be behind a door about here, but there's nothing but a solid brick wall."

"We need to get inside," Elwyn said.

Jude pointed her mobile this way and that. "Rachel's underground," she announced. "There must be garages, perhaps they're accessed at the back."

"You heard her," Elwyn told the team. "There's a courtyard in the centre of this building with a gated driveway from the road leading into it. There's about a dozen garages. Search the bloody lot of them."

"Elwyn . . ." Jude said. He was in danger of losing it. "You have no warrant. Shouldn't you tell Kenton what you're about to do?"

"Kenton's a fool. We need to get Rachel, and hopefully Jonny, out of there before Bain does them harm."

CHAPTER FIFTY

Holding on to Jonny for support, Rachel was kicking at the door. It was a futile exercise, the metal wasn't even dented. Her head ached, she felt dreadful and was running on nothing but terror. But there was no option, this was their last chance. Bain would be back any second and that would be it. He'd shoot them both.

Then she heard it, someone calling her name.

"Listen." She clutched Jonny's arm and shook it. "That's Elwyn. We're in here! Get us out."

"Stand well back," Elwyn ordered.

The next thing Rachel knew, a small piece of earth-moving machinery was ploughing through the door.

Elwyn chuckled. "All we could find. It was left down here from when this block was built."

"Help Jonny, he's tied up and can't move."

In minutes, Arran Copeland had Jonny free. "We've found Gilbert," the DC told Elwyn. "He's lying on the old sofa over there, dead. Looks like he's been shot."

"Have you brought armed response?" Rachel asked. "Bain won't hesitate to shoot the lot of us."

Elwyn shook his head. "Kenton. No help and no warrant. He firmly believes we're totally wrong about Bain."

"Give me your mobile and I'll ring him. We certainly need that warrant now, plus a full forensic team."

As she spoke, Jude appeared and smiled at her friend. "Just as well I fitted you with that tracker. You speak to Kenton, while I organise forensics."

"D'you know? What with the horror of what was happening, I completely forgot that thing. You're right though, it saved our bacon."

"There's someone coming," Arran Copeland hissed from the corridor.

Rachel retreated back into the garage and watched as Arran and the two PCs positioned themselves at the ruined door, ready to jump anyone who approached. They didn't have long to wait. Just seconds later, Bain marched up and stood staring at the earth mover. Rachel's heart was in her mouth. She'd had it, she wasn't up for more rough stuff. A mug of hot tea and an hour at her desk was enough for her. But Bain was no match for the officers. After a short tussle, Arran had him in handcuffs and had taken a revolver off him.

Bain's eyes blazed with rage. "Shame, I was looking forward to blasting your head off, bitch," he yelled. "I'd have done it too. Pay you back for all the trouble you've given us."

Rachel walked towards him. "Us?" she said. "Who're you working with?" Was Bain the mysterious 'Ghost'? If he wasn't, the man they most wanted was still out there.

"Like I'd tell you," Bain sneered.

"Okay," she said lightly. "You can take the blame for the three murders then."

"No!" he protested. "You can't do that. I didn't kill anyone."

"We only have your word for that." She jabbed her finger hard into his stomach. "You imprisoned my colleague and me in that black hole along with Jacob Gilbert's body. He didn't go in there and die of his own free will, and it is your garage. Comes with the apartment, I suppose."

"Not me, love. Someone with a far better motive." Wrestling with the officer holding him, he took a step toward Rachel. "Motive. It's a big word when you think about it.

Greed, what about that as a motive? That'd do for me, I'm all about the money. A quick return and get out with enough dosh to last me the rest of my life. But we're not all like that. Money means nothing to some folk."

"What do you mean?" Rachel said.

"So, if it isn't greed, what about revenge as a motive? Now there's a thought. You know what I'm talking about — the old eye for an eye and all that."

Rachel shook her head. "I've no idea what you're talking about. Never mind, you'll have plenty of time to explain yourself properly at the station." She nodded at the uniforms. "Take him away."

"There's an ambulance outside with paramedics ready to give you and Jonny the once over," Elwyn said.

"Thanks, but I'm okay. Let them take a look at Jonny, though."

"Ma'am, you took a nasty bang to the head," Jonny said.

"I'll take a couple of painkillers when I get back."

Rachel wandered off down the corridor, using Elwyn's mobile to call Kenton. It took her several minutes to make him see what was staring him in the face. "Bain is on his way in. I want him processed and putting in a cell overnight. Jonny and I have both been knocked about a bit so the interview will have to wait."

This time Kenton didn't argue the matter. He agreed to the warrant and said he'd have a uniformed officer bring it to her.

She went back to her team, who were watching her anxiously. "Right, everyone, we've got the go ahead to search Bain's apartment. Confiscate any weapons found. We're looking for anything that points to who he's working with. If anyone's got any bright ideas on who that might be, now's the time to air them. We need to close this case, but if Bain's not Ghost then we've still got a problem."

CHAPTER FIFTY-ONE

Bain's apartment was immaculate, not a speck of dust nor a single unwashed cup, and with the minimum of furniture. It was as if no one lived there at all. Rachel walked around each room in turn. "There's little in the way of cupboard space, so the search shouldn't take long. Right, Elwyn, you take the kitchen and I'll do the bedroom."

The bedroom contained nothing of interest, so Rachel moved on to the sitting room. There didn't appear to be anything here either, until she tried the drawers in the sideboard. One of them was locked. Tugging at the handle, she called to Elwyn, "We need to get into this."

He came in wielding a hammer. "Stand back, I'll hit it with this. Found it in a toolbox under the sink."

Minutes later the drawer hung open and the pair were going through the contents.

"Bills, receipts, just the usual boring stuff," Elwyn said.

"But there is this." Smiling triumphantly, Rachel held up a gold, diamond-encrusted crucifix. "If this is what I think it is, it proves that Bain did meet Sofia. Sofia told me she stole it from the Gilberts' safe along with the drugs and the lock of hair."

Elwyn held out an evidence bag and she dropped it in. "I can't find a thing to link Bain to anyone else. He has no diary, no notebook, no scraps of paper he'd written on. Nothing."

"We know he didn't work alone. He'll have his personal mobile on him and that'll be checked out. But we need to find any burners that might be lurking about. He'll have had at least one for contacting Gilbert, and then there's the dealers he'll have traded with."

Elwyn prowled around the apartment. "There's not many places he could have hidden such a thing."

Rachel went back into the kitchen and poked around in the cupboards. She noticed a row of six food canisters on a shelf, took one down and opened it. The label said 'Tea' but that wasn't what was inside. "Bingo. Look what I've found." She held up two mobiles. "What's the betting there's more in the other canisters."

"We'll bag them up and get them to Comms," Elwyn said.

"We need the results back quick, Elwyn. When we interview Bain tomorrow, I want us to face him with as much evidence as we can get our hands on."

"Let's go back to the station, get a cuppa and a bite to eat," Elwyn said. "After the day you've had, it's well earned."

Rachel gave a sigh. Elwyn was right. Tomorrow would be a big day, she'd need her wits about her, and that meant getting some food and sleep. "Okay. We'll drop the mobiles off first. Given what's happening tomorrow, I reckon I'll go home afterwards, get an early night and some painkillers for this headache of mine."

"You should have let the paramedics look you over."

"I'm okay, Elwyn, just a bit battered."

While Elwyn drove, Rachel leaned back in the passenger seat and closed her eyes. Something had been niggling her ever since they'd arrested Bain. It was what he'd said about motive. He'd intimated that the deaths were motivated by both greed and revenge. Bain was in it for the money, so who hated Gilbert enough to kill both his daughter and him?

* * *

Rachel returned to the station with Elwyn to pick up her car. An hour later, she pulled into her cottage driveway. First task, ring the kids. Belinda was a godsend but, poor thing, she'd had three kids foisted on her and Len was a force to be reckoned with.

"We're doing just fine," Belinda assured her. "Megan wanted to go and stay in her boyfriend's flat but Alan has had a word and she's agreed to stay here until you say it's safe."

"I hope it won't be too long. Another day or so."

Call over, Rachel showered, put on a loose tracksuit for comfort and, her face stuck in a report, wandered into the kitchen to find something to eat.

"We could go out if you prefer."

She spun round. "Jed! You have to stop doing this. You can't come here. The place is being watched. You'll get caught."

"That bother you, would it? Last time we met you gave the distinct impression that you weren't interested in what happens to me."

"Of course, I'm interested, but you cannot be part of my life anymore. It wouldn't be fair, either on us or the kids."

"How are they anyway? Little Len won't know me."

"And whose fault is that?" she retorted. "Look, Jed, I don't have the time or the patience for this right now. I'm on the verge of cracking a big case and I need to think."

"Anything I can help you with?"

"I doubt it. You're out of the picture where current Manchester villainy is concerned."

"Let me guess. You've been after a killer and now you think he's done for Jacob Gilbert too. You've found him dead and are trying to work out who'd have the balls."

He was right. "Apparently, his murder and two others we're investigating are down to revenge."

212

"One of those murders was his daughter, Emma, wasn't it? Apart from having unfortunate parents, she was a perfectly innocent girl who simply got in with the wrong crowd during the last weeks of her life. Not so her father. Jacob went through life making enemies, and one of them was always going to seek revenge."

"How come you're so well informed? Been reading my notes, have you, spying on me?"

"You're not the only one who can carry out an investigation, Rachel."

Her face fell. "Keep out of my case, Jed. I mean it. You can't stick your nose in and expect to get away with it."

He gave her a smile. "Pity. I was just about to give you a name."

CHAPTER FIFTY-TWO

Wednesday

Fired up by what Jed had told her, Rachel arrived at the station early the following day. She had important research to do before the others arrived. What he'd said last night had chilled her to the bone. More than that, if his information was correct, it should be easily proved.

An hour later, the others were gathered in the incident room awaiting her instructions. It was time to move.

Rachel's first words on joining them were to ask if anything had come in from Forensics.

"Unidentified prints on that old leather sofa in the garage," Amy told her. "Also, on the tarpaulin. Nothing to do with Gilbert, so it's a bit of a mystery."

Rachel wasn't surprised. Given what she now knew, that was only to be expected. This person did not have a police record. "Elwyn and I will interview Bain and I want a watch putting on St Paul's Church. No one must leave. We'll speak to the good vicar again later."

Elwyn stared at her, mystified. "Inside information," she whispered with a grin. "If I disclosed my source, I'd have to shoot you."

"Well, whatever you've learned and whoever from, it's certainly cheered you up," he said. "But I think you're wrong to go after the vicar."

"You'll just have to trust me, Elwyn," she said, suddenly serious. "I'm hoping it all falls into place but I'll know more later."

"Bain has hired some fancy solicitor, a Samuel Hirst from Hirst, Hirst and Laycock. They have offices in the city and aren't cheap," Elwyn told her.

"It doesn't matter who he's hired. Bain's as guilty as sin, Elwyn, and we're going to get the confession we need."

"And if he refuses to talk?"

"He won't." Rachel marched along the corridor heading for the interview room.

"Someone's told you something, something we didn't know before," Elwyn said, trotting after her. "You've been given inside information. Who've you been speaking to, Rachel? We don't have any informants who'd welch on Bain."

"It wasn't an informant, Elwyn, not in the accepted sense anyway. And I've no intention of telling you. My source is confidential and not up for discussion."

There was no way Rachel could tell Elwyn that her source was Jed. When she'd been in dire distress and afraid for her life, it had been Elwyn who'd helped her. He'd been the listening ear at the end of the phone, he'd let her stay in his parents' bungalow by the coast giving her time to recover. Tell him now that she'd even spoken to Jed, never mind that she was undecided about their future together, would be hard for her friend to take.

Rachel and Elwyn entered the interview room and sat down opposite Bain and Samuel Hirst.

"You're still under caution from last night," Rachel reminded Bain as she started the recording.

"My client has made a full statement," Hirst said, placing a sheet of paper in front of her. "He has nothing more to add."

"Not at all. There is a great deal more he can add," Rachel said.

Hirst gathered his own papers together and stood up. "I don't think so. Unless you've got solid evidence against my client, we're leaving."

"Tell me, Mr Hirst, how much solid evidence do you need? Mr Bain kidnapped me and a member of my team. He assaulted and imprisoned us both. The pair of us suffered head injuries inflicted by him, and had it not been for my colleagues, we'd still be incarcerated in that garage."

"I can assure you you've got that all wrong. Mr Bain has explained. Given the special nature of the job, he had to maintain his cover. Someone he knows to be a dealer had seen you with him and knew you to be a detective. Mr Bain had no choice other than to do what he did. His intentions were to leave you there for a couple of hours and then release you."

Rachel looked at Hirst's face, which had insincerity written all over it. "And the dead body dumped on the old sofa? What were his intentions for that?"

"That wasn't me," Bain said at once. "I just found him lying there."

"You're a policeman yourself, why not report it?"

He shrugged. "I don't know. I was going to deal with the body some other time."

"We spoke when you were arrested, remember? You told me then that you hadn't killed anyone, and that greed was your motive. You were in it for the money. You also said that the other killer was known to you. His motive, according to you, was something quite different: revenge."

Bain leaned forward. "I haven't killed anyone. Not Mary Dunn, not the girl, not Gilbert. I was locked in a police cell when the Dunn woman was murdered. You've no evidence that I had anything to do with Emma Gilbert's death or her father's." He threw his arms in the air. "Why would I? Gilbert was my source of income. Kill him and I'd have no more pay days."

Rachel hated to admit it but he was right. If his motive was greed, he had more to gain by keeping Gilbert alive.

"You know a great deal more than you're telling me. I know there are two of you working together and I want a name."

"I give you a name and it'll be me killed next."

"What if I tell you that I know who your partner is," Rachel said casually. "And that we're about to arrest him. It was easy enough to work out. What I don't know, however, is which one of you is 'Ghost'."

"You're lying. There's no way you've figured that out. You're a good detective but there's been nothing, no clues, no evidence at all."

"That's where you're wrong. We have evidence, both from the forensics and from our own deductions."

"You're lying. Come on, tell me, who d'you reckon you're looking for?"

"You know very well."

Bain laughed. "You're bluffing. Come on, admit it, you haven't a clue."

"You should be more concerned about the charges that will be levied against you. They run to a long list, Mr Bain, and will keep you behind bars for many years. Not a good situation for an ex-copper."

"Do you want to do a deal? My help in exchange for a name?"

Rachel watched him, the man was squirming at the thought of incarceration. He knew very well what that entailed. She felt Elwyn nudge her arm. He wanted her to accept.

"Sorry, you're too late. We know who we're after and we don't need your help."

"You can't know," Bain insisted.

Rachel looked him in the eye. "Ah, but that's where you're wrong. When we've finished here we'll be leaving for St Paul's Church in Ancoats where we'll make an arrest."

CHAPTER FIFTY-THREE

Rachel and Elwyn made their way back to the incident room in silence. She knew he was itching to ask her how she'd worked it out and above all, who had given her this 'inside information'. Just outside the office door, he suddenly stopped in front of her.

"You do know what you're doing?" he asked. "Only I haven't a clue what's going on. You can't really believe this is down to the vicar?"

"We missed something," she explained. "Staring us in the face it was, and I never thought to question it. And I should have done. It would have saved us a lot of trouble."

"What're you talking about?"

"That grave in St Paul's churchyard, the one belonging to Katie Neville." She gave him a few seconds to bring it to mind. "She was sixteen years old. The vicar made some comment about it being sad or something. Earlier this morning, I checked her death certificate. She died of a heroin overdose, Elwyn. Heroin supplied by one of Gilbert's people. She was in one of the county lines gangs Gilbert ran. Of course, there was no proof and no one was brought to book for it. The PM report made horrific reading. During her young life, that girl had been beaten, stabbed, and finally fed heroin until it killed her."

"What's her connection to the vicar?" Elwyn asked.

"I turned up something else too," Rachel said. "She was our vicar's niece. She's the daughter of his brother, George. You know, the quiet one, hovering around in the background, who looks as if he wouldn't say boo to a goose." She paused for a moment, looking steadily at Elwyn. "He's behind this, watching, and operating from the background. I firmly believe that he is 'Ghost'. I also believe that the good vicar, Henry Neville, has known all along and is protecting him. Time to tell the troops and then we'll go get him."

* * *

Rachel and Elwyn pulled up outside St Paul's in one car, Amy and Jonny in another. Rachel gestured for them to take the rear of the building.

"In case he decides to do a runner."

The pair went inside. The vicar was talking to an elderly woman and broke off the conversation to greet them.

"More questions? Inspector, when is this going to end?"

"Where is your brother George?" Rachel asked.

"What can you possibly want with him?" He sat down on one of the pews. "All this is getting me down. Surely you must be near the end of your investigations by now?"

"We are, but we need to speak to George."

At that moment Jonny appeared from the rear entrance. "There's an old estate car parked at the back, ma'am. It's the one I saw Bain get into in town. He had an argument with the driver before he collared me."

"What is this?" Henry Neville asked. "Surely you can't think George had anything to do with what's gone on?"

"Where is he?"

"He's in the cottage, packing. He's about to return home."

Rachel nodded at Jonny. "Troops arrived?"

"Yes, ma'am, don't worry. He won't get away."

"What is he supposed to have done?" Neville asked.

"I think you know very well," Rachel said, looking him in the eye. "In fact, I think you've been protecting him with your silence."

Henry Neville hung his head. "I'm not an evil man. George is my brother and he's weak. He never got over Katie and the need for vengeance ate him up."

"So, he paired up with Arlo Bain and the two of them set about fleecing Jacob Gilbert, finally murdering his daughter and then Gilbert himself. 'Weak', eh?"

Henry Neville sighed. "I couldn't stop him. I tried reasoning with him but the need to get even was too strong. He wanted Gilbert dead, and nothing was going to stop him."

She saw Jonny leading George Neville through the church in handcuffs. "I'll be right with you," she said. Turning her attention back to Henry, she said, "You'll have to come too, I'm afraid."

"But I've done nothing wrong."

"You knew what was going on though. You knew Emma Gilbert's body was down in the crypt, and that George had killed her. You might not have taken part, but you did nothing to prevent what your brother and Bain did either."

"Will I be charged?"

"That's up to the CPS, not me. If it was up to me I'd throw the book at you." She nodded at Amy. "Take him away and don't let him speak to his brother."

With the Neville brothers on their way to the station, it was finally over. Rachel gazed around her at the old Victorian church with its fancy stonework and stained glass windows. A shiver travelled up her spine. So much for being an oasis in a busy city. This oasis was dry and withered.

"Excuse me, Miss, is it all right if I do the flowers now?"

Rachel looked at the elderly woman and shook her head. "The vicar won't be back for a while. If there are any services today, I'm afraid the Reverend Neville won't be taking them."

"That's a shame. We were having a practice for my grandson's wedding."

"I'm sure the church will send a stand-in soon." Rachel smiled at her. But would they? If Rachel had her way, the building would be locked up forever.

"You ready for the off?" Elwyn asked at her side.

"I was just taking a last look round, but I'm done now."

"You never did like this place or the vicar, did you? Your subconscious tell you something?"

Rachel nodded. "It began here, Elwyn, on that Monday morning, and now it's come full circle." She took her car keys from her jacket pocket. "I felt it, you know, on that very first day. I knew there was something wrong here."

"By the way, Jude's been on. Her team have found evidence that puts Bain in the crypt. A thumb print would you believe — on the metal handrail at the bottom of the steps. Easily missed. She'll rush through the prints on the sofa and see if they match George Neville's."

"They will, I'm certain of it. According to his brother, he was eaten up with hate. That was his motive for killing."

"Back to the station, interview Neville and then a liquid lunch?"

Rachel gave him a smile. "Nice idea, but I fancy collecting the kids and spending the rest of the day with them. I need to let them know they can have their lives back. We'll speak to Neville in the morning."

CHAPTER FIFTY-FOUR

Thursday

"We still have a number of unanswered questions," Rachel told the team the following morning. "Why Mary Dunn had to die being one of them. She had nothing to do with Gilbert's trafficking or the drug dealers. And why Lawson's hair? I just hope that Neville will cooperate because if he doesn't, we might never get the answers."

Rachel wanted an end to this. This case was her first after her obligatory extended leave, and in her own estimation she'd not performed well. The final clue had been presented to her on a plate — by Jed McAteer of all people.

"You ready?" she asked Elwyn.

He nodded. "George Neville has hired Hirst, the same solicitor as Bain. They've been sitting together this past hour, no doubt concocting some weird and wonderful alibi."

She laughed. "Or we'll find a neat little statement waiting for us."

"I'm not sure what we'll get out of him," Elwyn said. "He could very well deny everything, point the finger at Bain and give us the run-around."

"Jude has processed the prints from the sofa Gilbert was found on. They belong to George."

"But we have nothing to link him to Emma's murder. Not one piece of evidence from the crypt. He could tell us anything," Elwyn said.

"The truth will do for me." Rachel marched out of the office, along the corridor and stood at the door to the interview room.

"His brother is here too," Elwyn said. "Henry Neville is waiting in reception."

"If he thinks he'll be taking brother George home any time soon, he's sadly mistaken."

The pair entered the room to find George Neville seated next to his solicitor. He looked pale and tired. He was a big man, older than Bain, and according to the disgraced detective, the brains of the operation. But looking at him this morning, Rachel had her doubts.

She wasn't looking forward to this. She had spent most of the previous night going over the questions she needed to ask. In the end she came to the conclusion that this first interview should be short, just long enough for them to find out how Neville was going to play this. They would then go from there.

Her first question was fired from the hip. "You murdered Emma Gilbert."

George Neville sat for a long time without speaking, his eyes darting from one detective to the other. Finally, he nodded and uttered a yes for the tape. Rachel closed her eyes for a moment in relief.

He sat up straighter, looking less weary. "Gilbert destroyed my daughter, Katie, and I swore I'd make him suffer in exactly the same way."

"Not content with killing Gilbert and his daughter, you also took the life of an elderly woman, Mary Dunn. Talk us through your actions."

Neville glanced at Hirst, who gave a little nod. "The old woman was in the church when I went down into the crypt and shot the girl. I had no idea she was there. When I went back up she confronted me, said she'd heard the gun going off and demanded to know what I was up to. I panicked and made up some story about dropping a metal urn and the sound reverberating but I could tell she didn't believe me. It was a Sunday evening after the last service was over. I turned to walk away but she stood staring after me, looking as if she wasn't sure what to do. I called Bain, and he said it was safer if she was out of the picture."

"What gave you the idea to arrange her body the way you did?"

"Bain. And after it was done, he gave me some hair to put on her clothes. He said it would confuse things for you lot long enough for us to get the girl out of the crypt."

He'd admitted to killing both Mary and Emma. Now for Jacob Gilbert.

"Not me," he insisted. "It's true I hated the man, more than anyone on this earth, but Bain beat me to it."

That was feasible — Gilbert had been found in Bain's garage — but how come Neville's prints were on the sofa? "But you were definitely in that garage, we have the proof. You must have known that Gilbert was dead."

"Yes, Bain shot him. Afterwards he rang me and asked me to meet him there. I wasn't sorry about Gilbert, just disappointed that I hadn't been the one to finish him."

"Are you prepared to make a statement saying that Bain shot Gilbert?"

"Yes, but I can do better than that. I can point you to the evidence."

Rachel was intrigued. "Evidence?"

"Bain told me Gilbert came storming round, looking for his daughter. He accused Bain of kidnapping her. The pair fought and Gilbert got knocked about, after which he took out a knife. He cut Bain's arm and it bled a lot. There has to be blood on Gilbert's clothing. That's your evidence."

* * *

"Will it be enough?" Elwyn asked as they made their way back to the incident room.

"The CPS will decide. But we'll be able to prove that the pair fought, which is something at least."

Rachel gave the team the good news. "He's made a full confession, but we still have a few loose ends to tidy up."

"Jude rang. Her people found another gun in that garage," Jonny told her, "and bullets to go with it. It was the gun that killed Gilbert and only has Bain's prints on it."

That was it then, all they needed to charge him. But why make such a blatant error? Bain didn't strike Rachel as being that careless.

"It was a small revolver, highly decorated, a favourite of his and special. Superintendent Kenton had a word with him earlier and told him it had been found. Bain got quite agitated. He asked the Super to look after it, said the thing had 'sentimental value', would you believe." Elwyn shook his head, smiling.

Rachel grinned. "I would, actually. Remember, Elwyn, these aren't normal people."

"What? The vicar?"

"Go and have a word," Rachel said to Amy. "Tell the man his brother will be staying with us."

Her earlier relief was growing. The case was done with, the killers under lock and key. There was just the paperwork to see to and that would be that. "Anyone wants me, I'm on the phone to the kids."

Disappearing into her office, she rang Belinda. "They can come home. It's finally over, villains caught and no more danger of kidnap."

"I'm glad. Len is missing you and Mia can be difficult when she doesn't get her own way."

"I'm sorry, Belinda. They're no picnic, I know. I'll be leaving work early and come to pick them up. What about Sofia?"

"I told her last night that you were nearly done. She's decided to go home. She'll speak to you herself later."

* * *

Rachel left the team propping up the bar in the station's local pub. Much as she wanted to join them, it was a long drive home and she had the kids to collect.

It had all turned out well but without Jed's help the outcome might have been very different. It had taken Jed to point her in the right direction and show her what had been staring her in face. It was doing Rachel's head in that she'd not seen it for herself.

EPILOGUE

For the first time in days, Rachel was cooking for the kids like she always did. There was even the usual spat between Mia and Megan about what to watch on the telly while they ate. Everything was back to normal with no obvious ill effects.

Sofia came into the kitchen. "There is a plane at nine tonight. I will be sorry to go but my mother is overjoyed at the prospect of having me back."

Rachel smiled. "I imagine she is. How are you getting to the airport?"

"A taxi will be here any minute."

Rachel patted her on the shoulder. "I'll miss you, and so will Len."

"He will soon forget. Thank you, Rachel, for taking a chance on me. I will forever be grateful."

Outside, the taxi sounded its horn. Rachel walked Sofia down the path. "Keep in touch, won't you? Ring or write, whatever suits." She waved at the departing car.

"You'll miss her," someone said over Rachel's shoulder. "Will you find someone else?"

Rachel turned to face him. "None of your business, Jed. You're not involved with the family anymore, remember."

"But I am. Two of them are my children."

Rachel glared back at him as he followed her inside. "Be quiet. Megan or Mia might hear you."

"Why shouldn't they? Mia, in particular, needs to know I'm her father and not Alan. Have you forgotten that DNA test you did?"

Rachel shook her head. "You really are a piece of work. And you wonder why I want nothing to do with you."

"Okay, no more talk of parentage. What have you decided about Spain?"

At that moment, Len came toddling in, clutching his favourite car. He took one look at Jed and ran towards him, squealing with pleasure. Jed scooped him up and swung him round while the little lad laughed his head off.

"He remembers you."

"I'm his dad, Rachel. Of course, he remembers me."

"Hi, Jed." Mia said, coming down the stairs. "I'm off to Chloe's," she told her mum. Turning back to Jed, she said, "You stopping long?"

"I'm here to invite the lot of you to my villa in Spain but your mum's not keen."

Rachel threw him a look. "Come on, Jed, it's not that simple."

"I'd love that. Half term's coming up too. Think about it, Mum. We haven't had a proper holiday in ages."

"Oh? And what about the three months in Wales? Or have you forgotten already?"

"Not Spain though, was it?"

Rachel knew she wasn't going to win this one, not now Mia knew. And once she came home, so would Megan. With the pair of them pecking her head, she'd stand no chance. "I'll think it over," she told Jed. "But if we do come it'll only be for half term, so don't go getting any bright ideas about it being a permanent arrangement."

Jed gave her a big smile. He didn't believe a word of it. "I'll be off then — things to do, people to see, and all that. I'll make the arrangements for the holiday. Who knows, Rachel, you might like it enough to stay? Make it that big change you're thinking about." And he was gone, closing the front door behind him.

Big change. She sighed. She certainly needed one of those. What she didn't need was Jed McAteer being so certain of what was good for her. And being so accurate.

THE END

THE JOFFE BOOKS STORY

We began in 2014 when Jasper agreed to publish his mum's much-rejected romance novel and it became a bestseller.

Since then we've grown into the largest independent publisher in the UK. We're extremely proud to publish some of the very best writers in the world, including Joy Ellis, Faith Martin, Caro Ramsay, Helen Forrester, Simon Brett and Robert Goddard. Everyone at Joffe Books loves reading and we never forget that it all begins with the magic of an author telling a story.

We are proud to publish talented first-time authors, as well as established writers whose books we love introducing to a new generation of readers.

We have been shortlisted for Independent Publisher of the Year at the British Book Awards three times, in 2020, 2021 and 2022, and for the Diversity and Inclusivity Award at the Independent Publishing Awards in 2022.

We built this company with your help, and we love to hear from you, so please email us about absolutely anything bookish at: feedback@joffebooks.com.

If you want to receive free books every Friday and hear about all our new releases, join our mailing list: www.joffebooks.com/contact

And when you tell your friends about us, just remember: it's pronounced Joffe as in coffee or toffee!

ALSO BY HELEN H. DURRANT

DETECTIVE RACHEL KING
Book 1: NEXT VICTIM
Book 2: TWO VICTIMS
Book 3: WRONG VICTIM
Book 4: FORGOTTEN VICTIM
Book 5: LAST VICTIM
Book 6: LOST VICTIM

THE CALLADINE & BAYLISS MYSTERY SERIES
Book 1: DEAD WRONG
Book 2: DEAD SILENT
Book 3: DEAD LIST
Book 4: DEAD LOST
Book 5: DEAD & BURIED
Book 6: DEAD NASTY
Book 7: DEAD JEALOUS
Book 8: DEAD BAD
Book 9: DEAD GUILTY
Book 10: DEAD WICKED
Book 11: DEAD SORRY
Book 12: DEAD REAL

DETECTIVE ALICE ROSSI
Book 1: THE ASH LAKE MURDERS

THE DCI GRECO BOOKS
Book 1: DARK MURDER
Book 2: DARK HOUSES
Book 3: DARK TRADE
Book 4: DARK ANGEL

MATT BRINDLE
Book 1: HIS THIRD VICTIM
Book 2: THE OTHER VICTIM

Manufactured by Amazon.ca
Bolton, ON